North by North Wit

NORTH BY NORTH WIT

An Anthology of Canadian Humour

Edited by Dale Jacobs

Thompson-Nicola Regional District
Library System
300-465 VICTORIA STREET
KAMLOOPS, BC   V2C 2A9

Black Moss Press
2003

National Library of Canada Cataloguing in Publication

North by north wit : an anthology of Canadian humour / edited by Dale Jacobs.

ISBN 0-88753-383-3

1. Canadian wit and humor (English)   I. Jacobs, Dale, 1966-

PS8375.N67 2003   C818'.607   C2003-902754-6
PR9197.8.N67 2003

Design by Karen Veryle Monck

Published by Black Moss Press, 2450 Byng Road, Windsor, Ontario N8W 3E8. Black Moss books are distributed by Firefly Books in Canada and the U.S.

Black Moss acknowledges the generous support of the Canada Council for the Arts and the Ontario Arts Council.

ONTARIO ARTS COUNCIL
CONSEIL DES ARTS DE L'ONTARIO

Le Conseil des Arts | The Canada Council
du Canada | for the Arts

Table of Contents

To: Black Moss Press
From: Dale Jacobs, Editor, North by North Wit
Re: Introduction

Okay, so here's the deal. I'm having a bit of problem writing the introduction to this collection. Okay, maybe a lot of problems. Usually it's the ending that's that's the kicker when you're writing, but when you're editing, it's always the introduction. Trust me. I tried not to think about it, tried to trick myself into thinking it would all fall into place. I was okay when we were putting together the call for submissions last summer, fine when I was reading through stacks of submissions, and not bad when talking to the contributors and editing the manuscript. But it was always there, lurking in the back of my mind. But this time, it's not only trying to write an introduction to a very diverse collection of work. No, this time I also have to factor in that it's a collection on humour. It's the introduction that's caught me again. What the hell am I supposed to say in an introduction about humour writing? Am I supposed to be funny?

Lots of false starts to report. Here's one that you might like in particular:

I like to laugh. Okay, so everyone likes to laugh, but I mean I really like to laugh, the kind of belly laugh that you makes you gasp for breath and brings tears to your eyes. Of course, I also appreciate a good chuckle or a serious guffaw or even the laugh that comes out as a snort. What really makes me happy is laughter that begets laughter. So, when I began to think about editing a volume on new Canadian humour writing, I smiled.

I was never sure I could sell the "laughter that begets laughter" bit with a straight face. What if someone actually asked me what that meant? So, a nonstarter there.

What about this one?

Laughter was coming my way in all of its myriad forms. The problem was that it never occurred to me that anyone would expect me to be funny in my introduction. Well, let me tell you right now, that's not going to happen. Sorry, but the funny introduction just isn't in my repertoire. I'll leave the laughs to the wonderful writers who follow.

Lame, isn't it? I'm not funny, but these fine writers really are. Trust me. I know something about humour. No, really, I do. See, trying too hard.

Here's another one:

The ground of Canadian humour has never been more fertile than it is today. In the next few pages, let me explain recent trends in Canadian humour that will help to situate what you are about to read. I will endeavour to trace the origins and current state of Canadian humour as precisely and definitively as possible.

To put it simply, yuck. Impossible task, lifeless prose. Here's a more honest version that underlies that one:

The ground of Canadian humour has never been more fertile than it is today. In the next few pages, let me explain recent trends in Canadian humour in the most humourless language possible so that I might sound smarter than I really am so that all of you will like me.

Maybe a bit too honest, that one. I like this next one; it gets right to the point:

You may be thinking, then, that my purpose in this introduction will be to examine the state of humour writing in Canada or to say something profound about humour writing in general. Wrong again. Nothing profound here at all. Nothing at all. Now go away and read the book.

Not right either. Too abrupt.

And then I had some notes that I never got around to doing anything with:

Lots of submissions
Lots of genres
Lots of approaches to humour
Lots of reasons to do the book right now
Lots of reasons to let the work stand for itself

See anything there you like? Just tell me and it's yours. Like I said, the main thing is that here I am coming up to deadline and I'm stuck on the introduction again. Worse yet, this time it's an introduction to a collection of humour writing. You see my dilemma. How did this happen? Is it too late to back out of the contract? Okay, just breathe and I can get this done.

So, you can see my conundrum. What do you do when you're editing a collection on humour and you're stuck with the introduction? You write a memo to the publisher and slip it into the front of the book. Now that's comedy.

Jay Dolmage

Imposing Order I:
The Laws of Robotics

Moose Lodge
Orillia, Ontario
November 3rd, 2002
Inaugural Meeting, Orillia Robotics Club

Well, AS YOU may or may not know, my name is Jaime Stevenson. You might have seen me some time or another down at the Radio Shed, which I happen to be the assistant manager of. Three years. Going on strong. I'm here today to talk about—what else—robots! The theme of my talk tonight is going to be The Laws Of Robotics.

My list of laws is important. That's why you need to pay attention. Of course, as far as robots goes, and my knowledge of them, I could take this to the top shelf, and up to the top intellectual levels, but I won't do that—even though I could. Instead, I'll cover the basics. Those things we'll need to know when we all have robots. Which we soon will. We'll all have robots *in the future*. And that's why we're having this meeting in the first place, to get ready to have robots. Correct?

Let me begin by saying that we don't actually sell robots at Radio Shed. At least not the good kind. Yet. We sell one that sharpens pencils. That's it. There's no walking and talking. But that's no reason to think Radio Shed isn't on the cutting edge. We are. We are very much on the cutting edge in terms of transistor radios, remote-control motorcycles and synthesizer keyboards, among other things. Just not robots, yet.

Let's face it, the robots I'll be discussing today may not really be invented. We're dealing with a hypothetical cutting edge, the kind of cutting edge we can only imagine. But this doesn't mean that we, as members of the Orillia Robotics Club, don't want to be prepared. We need to think about *the future*.

The first law of robotics.

When you are making a robot or having one made for you, you want to stay in control of how smart that robot is supposed to be. You don't want a robot that's way smarter than you. Because that would be annoying. But a dumb robot, or a robot pretending to be dumb, wouldn't be much better. They'd probably be dangerous.

Law two.

Teach your robot the difference between a good touch and a bad touch. There is a difference between tenderness and violence. If your robot doesn't understand that difference, I would say incapacitate and incinerate that robot. Don't try to recycle it. Or sell it used. You may ask, why would you want a robot that touched you at all? Well, I think some people would want that. That's all.

Three.

Keep an eye on your robot's vocabulary. You don't want your robot picking up words like "loser" to use on you. Or words like "marriage" or "get your own place" that your mom might program into your robot for it to use on you when she's not around.

Four.

Making a robot to take care of babies is not a good idea. Particularly if your robot also has a bread-maker. On account of the fact that a lot of babies are about the same size as a loaf of bread. And a new loaf of bread is about as warm as a baby. This is just common sense.

Law five concerns feelings. Robots can be friends. But taking it up a notch to another level is not a great idea. Traveling this particular road of loving your robot in a special way will lead you to a special dead end. This dead end is called 'it's a robot.' Which means it isn't a person, and not really real. Therefore, despite times when you are really confused and having complicated feelings towards your mechanical buddy, the robot won't love you back. At least it probably won't love you back. There may come a day *in the future* when we stock working robot hearts at Radio Shed. A pleasant thought, certainly. But something makes me seriously doubt it.

Six.

Please remember, a robot is *technology*. Technology is a double-edged sword and a two-pronged plug and a coin with one side and then another, flip side. As the manager of Radio Shed and a part of the Radio Shed family, I am well aware of this. Which is where I am speaking from my expert experience. Robot equals goodness, yes. But this goodness comes divided and then multiplied by a warning: your robot may one day replace you. Or be part of a robot uprising. Trust me, It could happen. I have an extensive collection of novels on the subject. On the other hand, of course, your robot could become your best buddy and confidante. Your robot could be the friend who's always there for you, even when you don't even feel like getting out of bed. But be careful. What I'm saying is keep an eye on the other edge and the other side and the other prong is all. Your buddy could be your enemy. Technology can go both ways. Which is why it's a can of worms that could open on either end.

I'll give you a moment to ponder that one.

Seven.

Don't put your clothes on your robot to disguise it. Don't send it to do things you should really do yourself. Like going to church with your mom, or jury duty. Because, really, that's wrong. You can't expect to get away with it. Especially under the eyes of God or a municipal judge. Be honest with your robot. Because are you a good person? As I mentioned, I've done my share of reading on the subject, and I can tell you that bad people shouldn't have robots, because bad things happen. Do you want to work for robots in a human slave camp? Think about it.

Okay, to summarize, I want to say that, in the end, all of these laws of robotics are important. And there are other laws not listed, of course. Because there are going to be so many robots and so many things to think about *in the future*. Bottom line, though, when all is said and done, is that if you are careful and thoughtful with your robot and with your approach to robotics, you will have a fun and useful friend that makes you less busy, less stressed-out, less messy, less hungry, less lonely, less friendless, smarter looking in personal appearance and cleaner in personal hygiene, less in need of a euchre partner for your mom's tournament, less worried about the build-up of dust-balls underneath the couch, less concerned about the maintenance of your car, less insecure around neighbors who thought that just because you are the assistant manager of Radio Shed you'd already have a robot, less obsessed with getting a robot because of your insecurity about not having one, less grumpy or gruff with people who previously seemed to change their tone with you when they found out you didn't have a robot, less likely to pretend you had a robot when you didn't and thus less likely to try and develop a robot voice to use when you answer the phone, saying,

"Just one moment please" with it when people ask for you, then making loud footstep sounds and then talking into your phone in your real voice as if you just came to the phone and then, later, asking whoever it is you are talking to to hold on a second while, in the background, but near the receiver, you have a fake conversation with your two voices. A fake conversation like this:

"Excuse me sir, would you like me to prepare you a nutritious snack?

"No thank you robot, I'm talking on the phone with a good friend."

"Yes sir, whatever you say my master, sir."

And if you have a real robot, you won't need to use a false robot voice, so then you'll be less likely, as well, to forget which voice you're using in a social situation. And less likely to, just by accident, ask for your plain glazed at the donut shop in the morning in the robot voice in front of a whole lot of people. And when you have a robot, even though you were an expert on them before you ever had one, you'll be even more of an expert because this is what you've been waiting for your whole life, and now the time is here when everyone wants to come down to Radio Shed and listen to what you have to say.

Okay. I did have some more things written down. But I'm going to end my speech here and say thanks to you for listening. Please do come back next week, and the following week. Attendance is going to be important. I'll be marking it down and keeping track of it on my personal digital organizer.

I'd also like to say that I'm available for extra consultation or for speaking engagements anytime. I can do a one-on-one session for you in your home. Also, please feel free to approach me after the meeting today. Or at any other time down at Radio Shed. Goodnight, and see you *in the future*.

Gail Johnston

Get-Ahead-Ed

Get-Ahead-Ed always works a few more minutes
after the rest of us down tools and head for home.
He's always the first one out of the shack;
he stands alone on the dock waiting
for us. He's always ready to go, always
on the job. He's gonna get ahead.

Ahead of what, Ed?
we ask him. *You get a head, Ed*
Buzz hollers, *Keep it under*
your fuckin' hard hat!

Ed's the kind the bosses keep
'til the bitter end of the job.
When the rest of us get laid off
and are back on the list at the hall
Get-Ahead Ed's still working – a real steady Eddie.

I love the look on Ed's face
when he gets pink-slipped
along with the rest of us,

but when the dispatcher says: *I just filled*
every request for a bridgeman,
on every single crew,
I know, tomorrow,
at the head of the line in the UI office
will be that fuckin' you-know-who.

B.D. Miller

Dumpster Diving:
A Comedy in One Act

Characters

JOE: a dumpster diver
GLORIA: a property owner

Time / Setting

Summer, the present. A back lane in an affluent neighbourhood.

(Lights rise on a back lane. A dumpster is centre stage with open lids and a sticker in front that reads: "All garbage must be bagged." We can hear flies buzzing. A shopping cart, half full of flattened beverage containers, is nearby. JOE is leaning into the dumpster, rummaging. Only his boots, legs and the patched bottom of his dirty jeans are visible. He emerges, whistling, with a plastic soda bottle in one hand and a juice carton in the other. He is wearing a grubby flannel shirt, with a canvas knapsack strapped to his back. JOE drops the bottle and carton on the ground, flattens them noisily with his boots and pitches them into the cart. He draws a pointy, four-foot stick from the cart, as if drawing a sword from a scabbard, and briefly pretends to fence. JOE chuckles and resumes leaning into the dumpster, banging the stick in the far corners, probing for loot. GLORIA enters, stage right, through a fence gate. Well dressed, she is carrying a bulging orange garbage bag with the thumb and index finger of one hand and is careful to keep the bag from brushing her clothes as she approaches the dumpster. GLORIA stops when she sees JOE, clearing her throat loudly. Startled, JOE drops his stick and bangs his head on the side of the dumpster as he straightens up too quickly.)

JOE: Ow! *(Rubbing his head.)* What's the big idea, scaring me like that?

GLORIA: What do you think you're doing?

JOE: What am I doing? .... Oh this. It's called dumpster diving.

GLORIA: Dumpster what?

JOE: Diving.... A respectable and profitable profession in these parts. Ever since the recycling levies of the early 90s.

GLORIA: You call rummaging through other peoples' garbage a profession?

JOE: Sure I do. Look, we've even got our own tools of the trade. Work gloves ... leather preferably. *(Pulling the stick out of the dumpster.)* Probe. *(Wobbling the cart by the handle.)* Cart. *(Turning his back momentarily to Gloria.)* Washable canvas knapsack. *(Pulling a flashlight out of his cart and shining it at Gloria.)* Flashlight ... for night diving. *(Returning the flashlight to the cart, pulling out a small plastic box.)* First aid kit. You'd be surprised how often you cut yourself in my line of work.

   (JOE puts the kit back in the cart.)

GLORIA: Tools of the trade. You're nothing but a scavenger!

JOE: Scavenger? Oh, you mean like the magpies. Pretty birds, them.

GLORIA: I think they're dreadful. And whatever you care to call what you're doing ... it is not permitted.

JOE: Says who?

GLORIA: Says the city, that's who. Can't you read? "All garbage must be bagged."

JOE: All the garbage <u>was</u> bagged. Even the grass clippings.

GLORIA: Precisely! And how much of the garbage is bagged now?

JOE: Well ... none of it anymore.

GLORIA: I knew as much by the smell. What's the point of people like me bagging our garbage if people like <u>you</u> come along with sticks and rip the bags open?

JOE: I gotta open the bags to get at the returnables. You know. Anything that pays a deposit. Pop bottles, milk jugs. Empty drink containers mostly. Once in a while I find other stuff too. Clothing. Antiques. Once I found a colour TV in perfect working condition.

GLORIA: You don't say. You know, the city passed a law that garbage should be bagged for a reason. To keep the air breathable for starters. *(Sweeping her free hand in front of her.)* And would you look at the flies! It's a matter of public health, that's what it is.

JOE: Well, if people like you would return your recyclables ... there'd be no incentive at all for people like me to open your garbage bags, now would there? *(Eyeing Gloria's bag.)* Speaking of which, looks like you got a couple of empty four-litre cranberry juice jugs in that bag. They'll fetch twenty cents apiece on return, you know.

GLORIA: How do you know what's in my bag?

JOE: I can tell by the bulges. You get a feel for that sort of thing when you're in the biz.... Jeez, that's a lot of cranberry juice. You got problems, you know.... *(Lowering his voice.)* With blood in your pee?

GLORIA: I beg your pardon!

JOE: It's just that I do a lot of reading while I'm out working. Old magazines and newspapers mostly. Whatever people throw out. According to *The Globe and Mail,* a sixteen-ounce glass of cranberry juice every day can reduce your chances of getting a bladder infection by up to seventy percent. Is that why you drink it?

GLORIA: I have no intention of standing in my back lane discussing ... urinary tract infections with a complete stranger.

JOE: Well, whatever you're drinking it for, the empties are worth twenty cents apiece.

(JOE steps back, so GLORIA has a clear path to the dumpster, and he sweeps an arm majestically between her and the bin.)

JOE: Go right ahead. Once you throw the bag in the bin, it's finders keepers!

(GLORIA retreats to the gate and drops the bag, facing JOE with her arms crossed.)

GLORIA: I think I'll wait till you're gone.

JOE: Okay, well, suit yourself. I'll just pick the jugs up later. On my way home.

GLORIA: In that case, I'll store the bag in my garage until morning.

JOE: What? Smell up your garage with trash, just so I don't get a couple of empty jugs? That's kind of a dog in the manger attitude, ain't it, Ms. Malloy?

GLORIA: *(Horrified.)* How do you know my name?

JOE: Oh, I get to know all of the people in my jurisdiction pretty well through their garbage. You can learn a lot from reading somebody's utility bills and credit card receipts, you know.

GLORIA: I don't believe this! You read people's private correspondence and financial transactions?

JOE: Well, it's hardly private if you just toss it into a dumpster, now is it?

GLORIA: Apparently not.

JOE: People should really shred most of that stuff. Might fall into the wrong hands…. The stories I could tell.

GLORIA: Stories?

(Pause as JOE smirks and the gears grind in Gloria's head. GLORIA steps quickly to JOE, lifting him by the back of the collar.)

GLORIA: What have you got on me, you little creep!

JOE: I don't got nothing on you, Ms. Malloy. Honest I don't. *(Beat.)* Well, nothing too bad anyways.

(GLORIA releases Joe's collar.)

JOE: I know you were born in '53. So that makes you—

GLORIA: I think I know my own age. What else?

JOE: Well, I know your husband left you a couple of years
            ago. I know that 'cause all of the bills were changed over
            to your name and I don't find any of his stuff no more.

GLORIA: What makes you think he left me? He could have died,
            for all you know. Then wouldn't you feel like a heel.

JOE: Well, I guess he could have died. But how do you
            explain all them invoices from Hooperman, Borowitz
            and Hinckley? (*In a booming voice, looping his thumbs
            under the straps of his knapsack, as if addressing a jury.*)
            Specialists in alimony, child custody, and matrimonial
            property law.

GLORIA: All right, all right. So I'm divorced.

JOE: I know you got two kids. Chelsea, sixteen, and Jayson,
            eleven. I find their stuff mixed in with yours. You eat
            Weight Watchers microwaveables at least four times a
            week. But it's kinda pointless on account of all the choco-
            lates, don't you think? You got quite the sweet tooth. And
            you're not big on fresh vegetables either … which I gotta
            thank you for, by the way. Nothing worse than rotten veg-
            etable slime when you're in my line of work. Snotties
            aren't so great either. Man, do I hate flu season.

GLORIA: Enough about your occupational hazards. The subject
            was me, remember?

JOE: Okay, okay…. You keep your house hot in the winter
            and cool in the summer. I know that from your energy
            bills. Whoppers, usually. And you use a lot of water.
            Although I'm not really sure for what.

GLORIA: I take a bath every day, I'll have you know. And my chil-
            dren shower regularly.

JOE: Hey, there you go. I thought that might be it. I find a lot
            of empty shampoo and bubble bath bottles in your

garbage. There's no deposit on those, but you should still recycle them.

GLORIA: So I don't recycle. Is that the worst you can do?

JOE: Oh, no. I'm just getting wound up.... I know you used to bank at the Commerce, but now you bank at the Credit Union. Some sort of a dispute over service charges if I recall correctly. Never less than one thousand in your chequing account, and a whole heap more in savings and RSPs. You've got a Platinum Visa, an Air Miles American Express, and a Bay card. You use them quite a lot, but you never carry a balance. Good for you! Credit cards are a killer if you carry a balance. Oh yeah, you got a Diner's card too that you use maybe twice a month. How was *Le Poulet D'Or* by the way?

GLORIA: The meal was adequate, but the service was a little slow.

JOE: That must be why you didn't tip! Usually you tip. About eleven percent on average. You're really supposed to tip fifteen percent, you know.

GLORIA: What would you know about tipping? You probably eat all your meals over the sink. Straight from a can!

JOE: Well ... if we're gonna get personal, how about your medical history? You're on Apresoline, I know that. For high blood pressure, I think. And you take Donnatal too. Helps prevent cramping in the bowels. You used to be on Prozac, but I stopped finding the pill bottles a few months ago. Congratulations, by the way. The new boyfriend must be working wonders on your frame of mind.

GLORIA: What makes you think I have a boyfriend?

JOE: Well, I don't want to embarrass you or nothing. But lately I been finding, you know ... jolly bags in your garbage. Usually on weekends.

GLORIA: Jolly bags?

JOE: You know. Love gloves. Shower caps. Jimmy hats.

(Beat.) Sausage skins. Willie wraps. Weenie beanies.

GLORIA: Wait just a minute. Are you insinuating there are used condoms in my garbage?

JOE: I'm not insinuating. I'm <u>telling</u> you there is.

GLORIA: When I get my hands on Chelsea, she won't be able to sit down for a month. She promised me they were only studying!

JOE: Well, hey, look on the bright side. At least she's using protection.

GLORIA: She's only sixteen years old!

JOE: Okay, well … at least she's not flushing them. That's hard on the plumbing, you know.

GLORIA: Is that a fact.

JOE: I could go on. About your profile that is. But that pretty much covers all of the bases, I think.

GLORIA: You know all that?

JOE: Yes ma'am.

GLORIA: Just from digging through my garbage?

JOE: Yes ma'am.

GLORIA: *(Slyly.)* What have you got on the others?

JOE: Oh, I couldn't rat out your kids, Ms. Malloy, that wouldn't be right. I feel bad enough about the condoms. I honestly thought they were yours.

GLORIA: No, no, I meant my neighbours. *(Pointing offstage left.)* What can you give me on the Roswells, for example?

JOE: I can't tell you that. I mean, it's one thing to tell <u>you</u> a bunch of stuff about <u>you</u>. But I'd be nothing but a snitch if I told you about somebody else.

(GLORIA steps to the gate, grabs her garbage and hurries to the dumpster, pitching the bag inside. She steps back to face JOE.)

GLORIA: There! You can have my juice jugs. And there's three wine bottles and about a dozen Pepsi cans in there too.

JOE: Hey, thanks a lot. But I still can't tell you nothing. Why do you want to know, anyway?

GLORIA: I've wanted something on Valerie Roswell for years. Ever since the wind chime incident. Now give me something I can use!

JOE: Sorry. Can't do it, Ms. Malloy. I'd be violating my Code as a dumpster diver if I told you.

GLORIA: Code? For the likes of you? There isn't any Code!

JOE: Sure there is.

(Anthem-like music rises.)

JOE: Like always clean up your mess and close the lids before moving to the next dumpster. If you knock stuff on the ground, then pick it up. Always be courteous when somebody questions you. Like how I've been with you. If a cop or somebody asks you to move on, move on. There are plenty of dumpsters to go around. Be discreet and don't linger. People think you're up to no good if you linger. If it takes you more than five minutes to go through an entire dumpster—even a commercial one— you shouldn't be in the biz. Don't make any unnecessary noise. Things like that. All part of the Code. Oh yeah, and any dirt you get on people in the course of conducting business, you keep to yourself. People like you are my clients in a way. That's how I look at it anyways. I'm obligated by the Code to keep everything strictly under wraps. No different than a doctor or a lawyer. I guess you could call it diver-dumper confidentiality.

(The anthem fades.)

JOE: So that's why I can't tell you stuff about your neighbours. But you know, Ms. Malloy ... there's nothing preventing you from getting the information yourself. First hand, so to speak. *(Gesturing at the dumpster.)* Be my guest.

2-4

GLORIA: If you think I'm going to resort to rooting through my neighbours' garbage—

JOE: Okay, well, suit yourself. But like I said ... the stories I could tell.

(Pause as GLORIA thinks it over.)

GLORIA: Step aside!

(GLORIA rushes to the dumpster, leans in and begins rummaging, emerging after a few seconds.)

GLORIA: Give me the probe!

(GLORIA grabs the probe and resumes rummaging, banging the stick in the far corners of the dumpster.)

JOE: *(To the audience.)* According to *The Financial Post,* two industries will enjoy unprecedented growth in the twenty-first century. *(Gesturing at the cart.)* One is recycling. *(Gesturing at GLORIA.)* The other is data mining.

(JOE begins whistling and pushes his cart offstage left, as GLORIA continues rummaging. Lights fade. The end.)

Jocko Benoit

In the Middle

This poem is in peak condition.
It has shaved .04 seconds
Off the time it will take you
To understand it. But the judges
Give it so-so technical marks
And almost nothing for artistic impression.
This poem glares at the Russian judge.
The French judge winks at it,
Warm for its form.

This poem tries again and again
But, several rewrites later, decides
To go back to being a poem.
It does not understand other poems –
How they often end in the middle.
Understatement is just another name
For giving up, it declaims.
This poem wants to win the Nobel Prize
And is disheartened to learn
It will need to join other poems to do it.
It tries to get a place in a big anthology
But settles in a small town magazine.

This poem revives the dream one day
And rewrites itself as a song
Which makes it all the way to #5.
It wins a Grammy, but not
The People's Choice award.
This poem is not happy
Just to be nominated. Its friends
Tell it that it can't be liked
By everyone. It stops answering
All their calls.

This poem falls in with a postmodern crowd
Who tell it that it never meant
What it thought it did – that no poem
Is better than another. They twist
This poem's words around the same way
Schoolyard bullies once ripped it
From a book because they didn't
Understand it, or because it said
Something that touched a nerve, or
Because they didn't like anything
They suspected might be smarter than them.

This poem had finally reached the past tense.
It felt dated and unremembered
Even though it had that one great line
Toward the end. It began to consider
Suicide. It threw itself from
The top of a building, floated down,
Was fined for littering. It tried
To throw itself into a shredder
But they were all busy eating
The evidence that capitalism may not
Have been number one after all.

For a while it found Christianity
That promised that all those who had been
Placed last on Earth would
Be placed first in heaven.
Talk about a comeback!
But all that stuff about a judgment day
Gave this poem stage fright all over again.

So it looked up that cute French judge
And it found out what's a metaphor –
To put a simile on her face.
And in the middle of one night,
In the middle of the French judge,
In the middle of its thoughts,

In the middle of its life,
In medias res the universe caught
Naked coming out of a meteor shower,
Every word in this poem's body contracted
Into the shape of a long moaned, "Oh"
Which swallowed space and time –
An ecstasy measureless to iambs,
Trochees, dactyls and spondees.
It was a moment large enough to fit
This poem's life inside. This poem
Rolled over and amazement dissolved
Into a confident smile. "So, of all the poems
You've ever had, where do I rank?"
The French judge giggled, but could not stop
The numbers from flashing across her eyes.

Jane Hamilton

Being Jane Hamilton

FIRST, NOTICE there is another Jane Hamilton, goddammit, who's just put out *The Book of Ruth*. Try to read *The Book of Ruth* but have trouble getting into it. Put it on top of *Ulysses*. Growl when it wins attention and prizes, because now, at best, you become "the other Jane Hamilton". "The Canadian Jane Hamilton." You can publish under your nickname, maybe, but it doesn't feel real, or under J.A., your initials, to avoid confusion. Decide on J.A. Otherwise, aren't people bound to say, "Jane Hamilton? Well, hello. I admired *The Book of Ruth* so much." Feel surprised by feminists who ask if you're pretending to be a man. Are you ashamed to be a woman? Do you think you'll get published more? Say yes. Say, That's why I did it. Heft your cajones. Snap gum. Say, Yes. Say, Hell, yes.

Publish a first book, a children's book, with a small west coast publisher. Attend a meeting about its upcoming trajectory. Your editor is praise-filled and excited, but his publicist is not. His publicist says, about the apartment building in which your character resides: "A bit of a cesspool, isn't it?" Your editor will quit the press just as the book goes to the printers; in the resultant upheaval, the publicist takes over and you do not get sent cover proofs. The book appears, to your mortification, with your nickname riding the cover. This is how you will be known to the Library of Congress now and forever, and, also, alas, to your six or seven readers.

Thank you, Jane Hamilton. You turn *The Book of Ruth* onto its belly, face down on *Ulysses*.

Call the publicist-now-editor. Complain.

"Oh, Jesus," he growls. "Without writers, this would actually be a pretty decent business," he says.

You publish a second book, a book of poetry with a small press in the east. You never intended to be a poet, but the editor was so complimentary when he saw some of your poems under a letter begging for a grant nod that you fell off the fiction wagon and landed on a pitchfork of line breaks. The press launches you east and west, sends you on reading tours, and otherwise makes you feel as good as a chocolate bar.

The manager of the press finagles a reading at a prestigious literary festival, which excites you even though, on the poster, you are listed not as Jena or JA Hamilton or even Jane Hamilton, your real name, but as JH Hamilton.

When you arrive at your publisher's booth, you scan their publicity flyer and notice it mentions *Body Rain* as shortlisted for a top poetry award.

"This isn't correct," you say to the business manager. You feel mortified all over again.

"Sure it is."

"I don't think so." You scowl.

"They sent me the announcement. Didn't I forward it to you?"

Well, no. No, she didn't. But what the hey.

The world is an exceedingly warm place, suddenly, where marvelous occurrences occur. You throw caution to the wind. You know you should read a short story but instead you read a non-fiction piece about having gum disease which is bound to appeal to the largely fetal crowd. About six out of one million people share your sense of humour, so you think it will be okay.

Afterwards, you hurry to the reading of a poet with hair. The festival takes place out of doors on the banks of a millpond, where a famously tall Canadian writer in a diminutive and properly battered boat poles his way through the shallows. You sit on your knees, because the bank is too crowded to spread out, behind two girls slightly down the rise. They are likely high school students; they are earnestly taking notes. In the middle of a sea of doodles, you catch your name (J.H. Hamilton), and one word in cursive caps gone over again and again till the pen broke through the page. It says, BORING. There is, however, a huge daisy asterisk beside it. Follow the asterisk down to the dregs of the page. Written there you see: Buy her book.

"What do you do?" someone asks at a party.

You admit you're a writer.

"A writer? What's your name? Are you published? Should I have heard of you? What do you write?"

You admit you write fiction and poetry.

"Anything I might have read?"

You shrug.

"Tell me one title."

"Body Rain."

"I've never heard of that," she says.

Although you have the same name as a famous Wisconsin author, you also have the same name as another local writer. One day you pick up the telephone. A woman says, "Is this Jane Hamilton?"

"Yes," you say.

"This is Peggy Dawson."

You have never heard of Peggy Dawson, but she goes on: "I'm really ticked off at you. Why did you leave the party last night?"

You are not entirely certain. You try to come up with reasons. A sudden stomach ache? A babysitter who needed to get home? Or maybe it was just because you don't like Peggy Dawson?

Your third book is fiction, short stories; a friend tells you that the house you settle on is planning to really get behind their fiction.

Fiddlefart around with the contract, but end up giving the publishers what they want: the world.

You admire the editor, who is able to pull your messy heap of stories into a cohesive whole. But it's the usual story: You want to include stories she doesn't like; she wants to include stories you wish you hadn't written. You squabble about the book's title. The editor likes one title, *The Names of Constellations,* and though there is a story of that name you hate it as a book title, but the only replacement you can offer is weak as watered down tea: *July Nights.* But that doesn't really reflect the book's content, the editor argues. "*Constellations* does?'" you say. You win, but when the editor calls you in to vet the cover, it's a red mess with a barely visible perfume bottle and a feather, and behind all that chaos, a map of the constellations. "You had this developed for your title," you say quietly.

"Don't be ridiculous," says the editor. "Doesn't it look like a July night?"

It is one of the worst covers you've ever seen. It looks like someone tragically ill has vomited on a July night. The editor makes it sound like ordering a redesign will force the publisher out of business. You don't care. You want them forced out of business if this is what they're doing with your book. You know you'll be embarrassed by this cover even ten years from now. But you capitulate. You tell her it's okay, that you'll live with it. You sigh and say, tragically, "Somehow."

The month *July Nights and Other Stories* is due to come out, you attend a writing workshop. There is another writer whose work you admire who also expects a book back from the printers. She wants to launch it during the workshop, though you hear such activity is frowned upon because it's not egalitarian. How very Canadian, you think, to ignore one person's accomplishment because others don't share it. Someone suggests that since you also have a book due, too, she ought to include you in her launch. Though it clearly makes her grit her teeth, the other writer asks if you'll join her. Well, you say, no way your publisher's going to spring for costs. That's okay, says the other writer, mine has already covered them. The other thing, you tell her, is that you already have plans that night, and you can't be back at the centre till ten past nine. Is that okay? Sure, she says.

Your book, of course, does not show up in time for the launch, but you are unruffled. You go off to your appointment. When you return, on time, the other writer is cranky. She tells you in no uncertain terms that you are reading first. Of course, you say.

You get through the reading using an old computer copy of a story since revised. People clap appreciatively. Then an attendee you barely know stands up to introduce the other writer. "Now," she says, rubbing her hands together gleefully, "the *real* reason we're here."

Your mother calls. She says, "Jane Hamilton's book just got chosen by Oprah."

Say, I know, Ma. Say, Thanks for letting me know. Say, I really appreciate it.

Your mother has never read your work. "Oh, Janie," she always says with an embarrassed giggle, "you're too smart for me."

You hear there is a porno star with, essentially, your name. Hers is Sarah Jane Hamilton. Your eldest daughter's name is Sarah Maya Jane Hamilton.

Wear low-cut shirts to parties. Crack gum. Stick out your hand,

and when people shake, say, "You don't know where this has been." Grin. Say, "Sarah Jane Hamilton at your service." Say, "Porn star? You may know my work?"

Someone says, "J. H. Hamilton. You're not *that* Jane Hamilton, are you? The one who wrote— What was it called? No, don't tell me. It'll come to me. You know the book I mean. What's the title? It's on the tip of my tongue. Okay, tell me. Go on, tell me. What, you don't know the title of your own book?"

You venture, *"Body Rain?"*

"Don't be ridiculous," says your interlocutor, frowning. *"The Book of* something. Rosemary? You wrote *The Book of Rosemary,* didn't you?"

You admit you're no longer sure.

The new publisher does not invest in ads for your book. It's listed in their catalogue, but how many booksellers are avidly scouting the press's almost non-existent fiction list for promising titles? You wonder how other people are supposed to know it exists, if they aren't told. Then it comes to you. Perhaps it is written in the constellations?

Your press tells you that book launches are a waste of money. But you stick to your pockety gums. You want a launch. You get a launch and it's a lovely, well attended event. You want to give oral sex to your entire audience, as befits a porn star, such is your gratitude. Hell, you would even give oral sex to your publisher—if they asked.

Some people evidently find out your book is out. They are called critics. The reviews are in, and weird. Have they read the book? Maybe not. Maybe they've read *The Book of Ruth.* Do you really write about crazy fabulist families scratching for fleas while they twist through windowless turrets, using menstrual pads to wipe the sweat off their hot-flashing faces while doing the dirty the gay way?

Okay, well, maybe you do.

It occurs to you that you haven't seen a royalty statement from your first press in years. Perhaps they are out of business? But no, the little dickenses have only changed their name to something pronounce-able. Where are your statements? The book was chosen for purchase by school libraries, so how is it that it hasn't earned a penny?

Lucky you read the newspaper, because *July Nights and Other Stories* is shortlisted for two literary awards and otherwise you wouldn't have known it. No one from the press calls, then or later, to offer notification or congratulations, nor do they follow up the nominations with publicity. You are flown to Penticton for the prize ceremony, which take place during a librarians' conference. Various librarians introduce the nominees. The fellow who introduces your book reads from the back jacket copy, then asks Mr. Hamilton to please stand. Perhaps you should have strapped down your breasts. You stand up grinning. If nobody knows it hurts, it doesn't hurt, right? Just like you don't get hurt when a tree falls in the forest and you're safe in bed.

Your reputation does not seem to be going anywhere. You're pretty sure it's not taking a plane out of the country, since none of your presses sells into the UK or US. It hasn't even hopped aboard the floundering Canadian Airlines to Toronto. You are positive it hasn't gone to Wisconsin. It isn't knocking on Jane Hamilton's door asking for a doggy bag.

Though you are regularly published and have won, now, first place in a few not insubstantial contests, you aren't asked to contribute to literary anthologies. Not of women writers. Not of Canadian writers. Not of lesbian writers. Not of disabled writers.

But that's okay. Reputations take time even for women with chronic and generally fatal illnesses like gum disease. Usually, reputations take major publishers and a firm commitment not to publish poetry. But poetry seems to be what you've compiled again, goddammit. You opt to publish with your same poetry press if they'll have you, because dealing with them was so good. Your editor loves your book. He thinks your poem "Immaculata" is the best breakup poem ever written, which just goes to show that you have a true talent for misery.

But you are stunned when the manager says, *"Lesbian* poetry? Will publishing this ruin our press?"

Will being Jane Hamilton ruin *you?*

Nothing happens. Being Jane Hamilton is at an all-time low. There aren't interviews or readings or many critical notices.

At your launch, two minutes before curtain, your publicist asks who's introducing you.

"Aren't you?" You are stoned on Ativan; you can't even see she's straight.

"I wasn't planning on it," she says. Then she says, "Oh, well, fine, if no one else will. Oh, all right. Give it to me," and snatches your copy of *Steam-Cleaning Love*.

She holds your poor benighted baby—its questionable cover and no doubt substandard poetry that is about to singlehandedly cause a press to go under—by its diaper as if it's just laid a big one and announces you've published "a bunch of other stuff" and well, here you are. Big whoop. Can we go home now?

Someone asks you to fly to Ontario to do a reading. After all the negotiating is over, the date firm, she calls and says shyly, waffling, "Look, I don't think it's— I mean I really shouldn't ask, but— I'm sure you're not, but— I'm sorry. I promised my boss. You're not the Jane Hamilton who wrote *The Book of Ruth* are you? Because if you are, Gloria says we can pay you more."

You get cheques from your first press, several cheques.

You are branching out, now, with a nonfiction book. It is a pseudonymous, commissioned work, for which, upfront, you have already been paid well enough to call the venture a success. The publisher tells you confidentially that he should be able to sell a press run of 5000 and, realistically, about 5000 copies a year for ten years running. You write the book in a record five months. You want cover blurbs, but the press tells you they're unimportant. There isn't time, they say. They call you up to say they're bringing you out in hardcover. They call you back to say they've reconsidered. Two weeks later—hardcover again. It goes to press as a paperback.

The publicity director of the press decides she can reach your specialty market via a clearing house she's discovered in Toronto, which sends out a monthly newsletter to all and sundry. They're balking about reading the book because it has no endorsement quotes, but the publicist vows to keep at them. She tells you, proudly, that she is putting all her eggs in this one basket, and that the review editor is bound to love the book if only she'll just read it. And she will, sooner or later, since the publicist is persistent. "I am," she tells you proudly. "I'm truly *hounding* her. It's getting to where she won't even take my calls."

The publicity director flatly refuses to advertise your book anywhere else. And then, without warning, she's fired. It's six months before the press signs on somebody new, and when you press this new person for publicity she says, "Are you crazy? That title is stale-dated."

Rights are nevertheless sold overseas and the book comes out in the UK. There is a flurry of press interest, but since you can't associate yourself publicly with the title—since they can't have an author photo, for instance—it quickly dies back.

The book is shortlisted for a UK award. Although your UK publishers can't spring for airfare, you could possibly cover that if only they would put you up. But they balk. They don't want to set a precedence for other authors by billeting you. Anyway, their books never win, they say.

The Canadian publisher takes you out for lunch. He commissioned the book because he had the same problem in his family that you had in yours. He tells you how important the subject is, how critical your book is.

You say you should have had an agent. An agent might have sold this book into the US and it might have gotten to the people who need it.

He says, "I have a great idea. Why don't I give you back the US rights and maybe you can make a sale yourself?"

A month later, when you bump into him at a party and ask him whatever happened with the US rights, he blows up. "Don't you think you can order me around!" he cries. "I won't be manipulated!"

That Christmas, your book appears on a UK list of best books of the year—alongside Roddy Doyle et al, after which it's remaindered.

You meet a friend downtown for dinner with a writer who publishes with your latest publisher. She says, "I think I know your name. Didn't you publish *The Book of Ramona* or something? Were you at the Christmas party?"

You are mortified—again. You weren't even invited. You say, "Well, no, you wouldn't have recognized me. I went as a porn star."

It's humiliating. The next day you call your publisher and ask him why you weren't invited.

"It was just for this year's authors," he says.

There is a pause before you manage to tell him you were this year's author.

He is apologetic. He swears it will not happen again. Send us your current address, he says.

You do, by regular mail. By registered mail. By singing telegram. You even rent a light plane and have it buzzed across the sky above your publisher's office. The next year, you get your invitation six weeks after the party. It is the last one you ever receive.

You really, really want to just call yourself by your actual name: Jane Hamilton. But the original, Wisconsin, problem has published to even more success now. After researching a family memoir, you decide to throw in your grandmother's birth name between your names, and you become Jane Eaton Hamilton.

You agree to participate in a group reading. You need a short piece. You have a comedic story in your collection called "Blood" about two girls who think a friend of theirs may have gotten her period. About three minutes in two older women in the front row stand up, shake their heads, say "tsk" loud enough for everyone to hear and walk out.

You meet a very famous Canadian Author at a party in Toronto. An important anthology of international lesbian fiction has just been published, with an entry by her. You tell her you wouldn't mind her inclusion if she were a lesbian. You tell her you wouldn't mind her inclusion even if she was straight but had written a lesbian story. But a straight woman with a straight story in a critical lesbian anthology? It just takes up a space an actual Canadian lesbian could use. She disagrees.

"Look, if the editors think my name will help sell books, I'm happy to help."

Back at home, you pen her a note. You tell her you are sorry you disagreed; that you've been an admirer of her work over the years and just wanted her to know that.

She writes back. "We didn't have a disagreement," she says. "Merely you had an opinion, and I did not."

Your mother calls. "Another book of Jane Hamilton's was chosen by Oprah. I just thought you should know that."

Say, Hey, thanks a lot. You just made my day.

You sit on a jury for a fiction prize. The three-member jury awards the prize to a young writer who published a volume of short fiction. After the ceremony, you make a point of seeking her out to congratulate her.

"You've published how many books?" she asks. "Four, right?"

You are a bit baffled. Five, but why is she counting so closely?

Steam-Cleaning Love came out the same week as my book and we launched at the same venue," she says. "You were Tuesday and I was Saturday."

"That's right," you say. You vaguely remembering signs announcing her launch, though at that point you weren't familiar with her work.

"Know how come I know?" she says and takes your elbow.

You shake your head. Shouldn't she be happier, you think? Shouldn't she be pleased she won?

"Because a bunch of the people at your launch were only there by mistake. They meant to come to mine instead."

You get email telling you about a web site for "TEEN BUTTS". Either somebody has been following you and knows how much weight you've gained and is poking fun, or it's mail for the pornographic Jane Hamilton.

There is a message from a powerhouse New York editor. You are not in your office when it comes in, and it so discombobulates you—is the sound in your chest the noise of your ship docking, rubbing against pilings?—that you wait two days before responding. You go over every project you've published in the past—does she want to acquire US rights?—and every new project she might have got wind of, but you are still baffled.

"Prestigious editor, please. It's Jane Hamilton returning her call."

The receptionist can't get her on the blower fast enough.

"Jane? Is that really you? I'm so sorry to bother you. I hope you don't mind me bothering you. Do you mind me bothering you?"

Do you mind her bothering you? How are you supposed to respond to that?

"Did you get the book I sent?"

You haven't received any books.

Hotshot editor laughs. "Of course you haven't. I just mailed it. But tell me. Do you ever do book reviews? Because this is a very worthy book."

"Sometimes," you say. You admit you prefer not to.

"Well, maybe you'd want to this time? If you really, really love the book I've sent, would you?"

"Perhaps, sure." But you are awfully puzzled now. Can you also, perhaps, kiss her feet? Give her a massage? Clean her toilet?

"Listen, Jane," she says and rushes on. "Let me tell you something everyone here and I mean everyone is just wild for your work we can't get enough some of the staff report that it's kept them up nights it's so important so real so poignant so touching so wonderful so completely over the top astonishing do you know that God you are a fine writer the real deal the real McCoy I hope you're proud of all your accomplishments we're just so excited to be publishing *The Book of Ruth*—"

Wait just a damned minute here. *The Book of Ruth?* What is the sound of one hand clapping? What is the sound of a one writer dying? If a writer dies alone in her office and nobody hears her is she really dead?

"—I just have to say again how important and wonderful this book is—"

How exactly can you cut her off? When you don't want to? When you want to pretend, just for a minute, that the praise—embarrassingly deferential though it is—is meant for you, and will sustain you through writer's blocks and slights? When you can't slide a word of protest in edgewise? There's the noise of all that unbreakable praise, and muddled in with it, the sound of your nautical emergency, your boat sinking fast, water pouring in over the gunwale, the scramble for life jacket, the farewells to your beloveds— "Uh," you say. "Uh, goddess of publishing?"

"—what a classic character you've created in—" She stops, thrown off. "What?"

"I really admire *The Book of Ruth* too—" You really have to try to read it again and see if you can get through it. "—but I have to tell you, I didn't write it."

"Of course you did," she says.

"No, I really didn't," you say. It is long since true, though, that you wish that you had, since the countless compliments you've had to deflect about it have left actual pock marks on your skin.

"Who am I talking to?" She's pissed now, as if you pretended to be someone you're not.

"Jane Hamilton. The Canadian Jane Hamilton. Jane Eaton Hamilton."

"The Canadian Jane Hamilton?" she says crankily, all obsequious-ness vanished. "There's no Canadian Jane Hamilton."

Tell me about it. "Really," you say, "there is."

"How did I get your phone number?"

"I have no idea."

"My secretary obviously gave me the wrong phone number."

"Yes," you say laughing.

"I'm glad you think this is funny."

"It is funny," you say, because it is extraordinarily funny in its sad, pathetic way. Like your life.

"I guess you'll be getting a book from me," she says curtly. "Just send it back, will you?"

Later that week, the book arrives, a hardcover nonfiction title you've never heard of, but you don't send it back. One lousy book? Cripes, it's the least a famous editor can do. If she had any decency, she'd also have asked to consider one of your manuscripts.

You give a party at your house celebrating a friend's engagement. Her fiancé, an Intensivist at a local hospital, tells you at length about his job. A while later it occurs to him that he's been monopolizing the conversation.

"What do *you* do?" he asks.

You say, "I'm an author."

His face blanches. He rears back. He swabs his face with his hand. He says, "Did you just say— You just said you're a *nothing?*"

Some days your in-box has more mail for Sarah Jane Hamilton the porn star than for you. Some days your in box has fan letters asking whether the main character in *The Book of Ruth* is really someone from your own family. "Did you base her on yourself?" the letters ask. You are tempted to write back and say no, you based her on Sarah Jane Hamilton, the porn star.

You finally read *The Book of Ruth,* which, as the text proceeds, you admire more and more.

You get lists of the search words used to find your web site. Jane Hamilton, Jane Hamilton, Jane Hamilton, they read with boring regularity, until one week they are enlivened by NAKED JANE.

You understand how bad it's gotten when you start feeling sorry for friends who have books coming out. For the regular folk, whose books may or may not be a cut above but who are nevertheless going to get treated like yesterday's fish, you feel sorry. You know they are likely to be heartbroken when they aren't shortlisted for prizes; when they aren't reviewed; when the reviews they do get are poor. You know they are likely to be crushed like garlic in a press by their colleagues.

You go on writing. You go on winning contests. You put together two short story collections. You sign with an agent in New York. You finally finish one of the novels you've been teasing along for years which you ship to your agent, who reads it and reports that it's smart, sharp, funny. But she also says that it's unfortunately midlist and probably—well Jane, she says, the thing is—I'm pretty sure this is going to be a tough sell.

You sit back and wait for—yes—nothing to happen.

Elizabeth Glenny

Sans Lemon Grass

This morning the food editor wrote,
"Dump the cilantro,"
touted getting back to basics,
find flavours in simple dishes
naked potatoes scrubbed and baked,
medallions of loin still resembling meat
not inukshuks rising from the plate.

Imagine dining sans lemon grass,
supper without Italy's shapely pasta
cloaked in asiago and garlic,
parmesan dabbed in fusilli,
never again crushing
threads of saffron.

Years of bedtime reading
wasted on haute cuisine,
hours tying muslin
sachets of bouquet garni.
No more soupçons of this or that.

My eyes roll heavenward to
the wrought iron chandelier
purchased to beam
on Athenian grape leaf wraps,
destined to glare on spuds and turnips.

Roger Bell

Bylaw

JOSE LIBERTAD crouched under his desk in the basement suck-ing hard on his cigarette and watching the stubby stockinged legs of Mrs. Mackenzie go back and forth past his window. Even though it was summer, she wore thick, droopy, opaque hose. He couldn't see her higher than her knees (didn't want to, really, his gorge ris-ing at the vision of flabby, dimpled thighs) but he could imagine her slack arms and her puffed face, pug nose aloft, sniffing eagerly around the foundation of his house.

"She's still out there!" he yelled to Florence, who was in the next room ironing clothes.

His wife dabbed at a collar that insisted on puckering. "Oh stop being so paranoid, Jose." She increasingly felt like a mother trying vainly to wipe a smear of strawberry jam from the pursed mouth of a squirming child before the kid returns to school after lunch. She had no children, so where did that thought come from? Actually, in a way, she did. Jose was petulant child enough for any woman most days. "She can't possibly smell anything. Garrett guaranteed that when he put in the Super Clean Ionizing Filter; not one molecule of cigarette smoke can get outside, that's what he said. She's just snooping for snooping's sake; that's her nature. Since old Alex died last year she has no life of her own and needs to live others' lives, that's all. Just pull the curtains and ignore her."

But how could he ignore her? Now Mrs. Mackenzie was down on her hands and knees peering in the window. How he wished he could be outside, stealthily approaching that raised rump. How he'd love to boot her assbones, drive her permed grey-haired head through the window glass, maybe have the good fortune to watch a stray shard slice her carotid, see those stumpy legs kick vainly as her horrible black blood escaped her in spurts. Jose shrugged him-self further back into the recess below the computer, happy that the keyboard slide was pulled out.

That would help obscure him from the old witch's invading eyes. He stopped dragging on the cigarette, afraid she'd spot the glow of the tip in the shadows where he hid. The bright sunlight in which she crouched and the gloom of the basement conspired against Mrs. Mackenzie. She vainly cupped her hands against the glass and willed her eyes to adjust further but her pupils balked. Reluctantly she pulled back, shoved herself, grunting, to a standing position, dusted off her hands and knees and strode away.

He waited a minute more, just to be sure (she was after all, a tricky old bag) and stiffly extracted himself from his cave. He yanked the curtains tight, shutting out the day and the possibility of any further spying, and sat back down at the computer. He tried to return to the poem he'd been composing. But he was blocked now, really and truly bunged up, like a colon that hasn't had the benefit of roughage for days. Goddamn that woman! Goddamn all the do-gooders, the health freaks, the protectors of the self who had made his life mis-erable with all their proselytizing and their rules. He regretted the day he'd come to North America. Back in Barcelona he could be strolling the Ramblas right now, smoking openly, throwing the butts on the ground when he was done with them, grinding them satisfy-ingly with his heel into the public pavement. He poked tentatively again at a few keys but it was still an unsuccessful attempt; nothing was moving. He shut down the machine with a savage series of dry grunts and strode in to complain to Florence.

Who was lost in the Zen of ironing, smoothing out all life's little troubles with her Magic Steam. And thus was not particularly appre-ciative of Jose's whingeing intrusion, nor as sympathetic as he'd have liked her to be. "I don't know why you don't just quit, any-way. Most people have. I mean, it's been illegal now to smoke, even in your own house, for four years.

Look what you've cost us with all these special filters. That Super Clean alone was nearly ten thousand dollars. And the cost of ciga-rettes on the Black Market. I mean, what pleasure can it give you to be a fugitive, an outcast from society? Why do you have to smoke? Is it the same reason you have to have a dog? To be contrary?"

Jose picked at a chunk of tobacco between his teeth with his tongue, meditatively, spat it out. Florence winced, slipped a piece of recycled paper toweling from the laundry room dispenser, bent, swiftly wiped up the tiny piece of leaf and deposited the mess in the compost container alongside the dryer lint. She went back to ironing. Jose seethed. "See, even you monitor my bad habits. Shit, they are *my* habits still, aren't they? How are they hurting others? Ok, if I can't smoke in public, well, I saw that coming with all those prissy-ass laws, but why not in my own house? Is this my domain or not?" Florence pretended he wasn't there, studiously ignoring the "my" with which he'd preceded "domain"; she admired the sleeve she'd just smoothed. He repeated, "Is a man's home his castle or not?"

"Not," replied Florence. "Not any more. That's an antiquated, patriarchal, twentieth century idea. The Bylaws were enacted to protect the vulnerable, that's me, non-smoker. Protect me outside the home *and* inside it."

"But you don't need protection, Florence, not from me. You've never objected to my smoking, not in Spain, not here."

"No, true, I haven't, though I have to admit, what I found romantic on the Costa del Sol I find less so now. But what if I were a little kid, your kid, and had no power, and you insisted on smoking around me? Clogging my little lungs, strangling my cilia with those smokey fingers? ("Hmmmm, not a bad metaphor," thought Jose, who filed it away for future use.) That's why the Bylaws were enacted, why the enforcement's so strict, why the penalties are so severe. To protect those who can't protect themselves."

"But you *aren't* a child and you *can* protect yourself. And we have the *Filter.* And it's *my* goddamn house which I bought and paid for with *my* goddamn money and where I should have the right to do *whatever I goddamn well please."* His voice rose so much into a plaintive wail/rant that it brought little Pepe skittering from his bed to see what was wrong. He stood looking up at a perturbed Jose twisting an unlit cigarette into shreds which Florence was frantically sweeping up as fast as they floated to the floor. Pepe, as he awoke, became attuned to his little dog body and realized suddenly he'd been asleep hours and had to pee and poop badly, so he bounced kinetically, yipping around Jose's legs. Translated: take me out, before I explode.

"Please walk the dog, will you. And don't forget to leash and muzzle him. Jose?"

"What?" He calmed his agitated hands. "Yeah, yeah, okay," he said, the anger beginning to recede into resignation. Then it swelled again, a fresh tsunami of resentment. "Leash and muzzle *my* dog in *my own* back yard. Holy Mary Mother of Jesus, where's the justice in *that?*" And he so swiftly plucked Pepe up off the floor and swept him up the stairs that the poor dog had no chance to tighten his sphincters and thus dribbled some pee along Jose's arm, which brought on another string of cursing and a slap on the head for Pepe, which brought on another dribble, and so on.

Florence dabbed at the urine-tracked carpet with some CleanAll and sighed, awaited the slam of the back door as a signal that peace had returned and she could get back to her Magic Mist. The thwuck of door on frame came and quiet descended on her world once more. She began to hum and drift and each little spritz of steam into the fabric was like a tonic for her wrinkled nerves.

The backyard sunlight nearly blinded Jose and Pepe. The man set the dog down and both stood uncertainly trying to adjust to the solar onslaught, but Pepe had little time to allow for adjusting, given the imperative of his bursting bladder and bowels. He quickly led Jose by the leash over to his favourite spot, a portion of cedar hedge separating the Libertad property from the Mackenzies'. He balanced expertly on three legs and unleashed a hissing stream onto the hedge, then, apparently satisfied with his work, moved away a few paces, circled twice, as if seeking sanctified ground, and squatted, where he evacuated several turds that seemed impossibly large for such a small dog. Jose watched the dog's eyes glaze over with the satisfaction of unleashing stools of such magnitude.

Jose had an almost overwhelming urge to light up, to sit down in the sun on the lawn, to fill his mouth and lungs with smoke, to glaze over with uninhibited pleasure the way Pepe had done. But he felt the Bylaws around his neck like a collar, one of those electronic collars they fitted criminals with these days to track them. Pepe stood erect, stiff-leggedly scratching a few ineffectual tufts of grass and dirt up over his dungheap. He looked up at Jose from behind the ludicrous muzzle to tell his master he was done. Jose bent swiftly down and unfettered his dog's snout, for which Pepe rewarded him with a generous lick.

Jose turned back towards the house with his companion, had walked no more than three steps when he was stopped by a "harrumph" from the gate in the hedge. He turned to see the dour Mrs. Mackenzie pulling unhappily at her apron. "Mr. Libertad, you're not leaving that excrement there, are you? You're required by law to clean it up, you know."

Jose launched a hard stare at her. At his feet, Pepe growled at Mrs. Mackenzie, who nervously stepped back. Jose moved his tongue against the sharp tips of his canine teeth. He knew what Pepe was feeling. Something primitive and unspeakable. Oh to sink fangs into the quivering mass of her third chin and shake her like a mongoose does a snake. He took another step towards the hedge, luxuriating in the fear in her eyes as she backpedalled. Then he turned sharply away, dragging a still rumbling Pepe with him, returning seconds later with a rake and round-nosed shovel, which he used to corral the offending turds. He carried them deliberately to the garbage pail, all the way feeling her watchful eyes on his back.

Another "harrumph" made him swing back to her. "You do know," she said slowly, as if to a thick child, "that all animal excrement must be disposed of through the sewage system, where it can be *properly* treated." She had emphasized "properly" for his edification. "Regulations prohibit it being placed in household refuse. Surely you know that, Mr. Libertad." She balled up her fists righteously.

Jose gripped the round-nosed shovel with both hands and closed his eyes, trying to regulate his breathing. He could imagine the half-dozen swift strides to close the gap between him and Mrs. Mackenzie, the way she'd gasp, step back to flee, fall heavily, try to rise then ineffectually raise her arms to protect herself, the sort of swing it would take, the arc of the metal head, the turds being flung centrifugally, the flat thwack of the shovel against the old woman's skull, the porridge of brains. It might be worth it.

But Florence picked then to emerge, having set out in search of her husband, who'd been gone too long given his dangerously agitated state when he'd left. She could smell the heat lightning tension, saw the way Jose's knuckles had whitened on the ash shovel handle, took in the combative stance of Mrs. Mackenzie, who was still sounding her knowledge of the Bylaws like a bagpipe. She'd better defuse this right away.

"Good afternoon, Mrs. Mackenzie. Magnificent weather we've been having?"

Mrs. Mackenzie relaxed her defensive posture. She always felt better in the presence of Mrs. Libertad.. Her neighbour's Spanish husband appalled and frightened her with his continental carelessness and his dark angry eyes, but Mrs. Libertad, having been born and raised in this country, seemed civilized. "Yes, yes it is. My tomatoes are loving it. They're healthier this year than any year I can recall. All this dry heat, I suppose. Although the green beans aren't happy."

Florence had positioned herself between the combatants and Jose saw that it was over. He swallowed bitterly and entered the house to flush Pepe's poop down the toilet. As it swirled away he felt like it was his rights that were being sucked down into that Stygian hole.

• • •

AN OPEN DOOR was the beginning of the escalation. After dinner, Jose, having seen off Florence, who had left for a clothing care seminar at the local library, went outside to drink his coffee, to sip it along with the last benevolent rays of the sun. But he didn't push the door shut properly, and Pepe, once again needing relief and finding no Jose to take him out, grew tired of waiting and tentatively nosed the door, which popped open, much to his surprise and delight. Out he stepped, past the oblivious Jose who was sprawled on a chaise lounge savouring his dark roast and imagining a fat smuggled Cuban cigar to go with it. Pepe looked to the gate in the hedge, and it too was open! Undiscovered territory beckoned Pepe the leashless and he responded like any true explorer: tail up, tongue out, eyes sparkling with adventure he entered the uncharted territory of Mrs. Mackenzie's yard. Among the tranquility of her Bonnie Best tomatoes it felt favourable to stake his claim so he planted himself and evacuated, almost sighing, if dogs can sigh. But his pheromone-induced euphoria gave way suddenly to pure pain as Mrs. Mackenzie's solid practical black brogue connected with his haunches.

Jose heard the dog yelp, sat up too suddenly, choked on his coffee, which burned its way out his nostrils. He leapt up and, still gasping, made his way towards his dog's cries, which were suddenly replaced with human howling. As he pushed through the gate he was greeted by a dervish, Mrs Mackenzie shrieking and whirling, periodically swinging her right leg as she tried frantically to disengage Pee, who was clamped onto her ankle just above the offending brogue. What he gave up in size Pepe certainly won points for on tenacity. Despite her thrashing, he couldn't be dislodged. The coffee-stained Jose stood gawping for a moment then began to laugh, which was the beginning of the end of Pepe's amazing ride, for the derisive laughter so infuriated Mrs. Mackenzie that she experienced a fresh shot of adrenaline. It propelled her towards the garden shed where she grabbed her garden hose and blasted the chihuahua with a burst of cold water. The dog was mad but not enough to drown for revenge. He let go and hightailed it out the gate.

Panting, dishevelled, soggy, Mrs. Mackenzie turned her fury on the smirking Jose. "Dog off property unattended," she rasped, " Bylaw 241a. Dog unmuzzled and unleashed, 241c." He noticed that her stocking was torn at the ankle, and that she was bleeding might-ily from Pepe's tiny incisors. Her face was an ugly purple. "Dog bites, 241g. Dog defecates or urinates on property other than owner's, 241e…"

Jose chimed in, stopping her short: "Feces not cleaned up and disposed of by dog owner, 123456w," he mocked. "Let's look after that, shall we Mrs. Mackenzie?" And he bent down among the thriv-ing Bonnie Best, scooped up the still warm turds in his bare hands and, baseball style, wound up and flung them against the white alu-minum siding of Mrs. Mackenzie's neat bungalow, where they spread on impact, leaving the siding an abstract painting of rage and yellow/brown flecks. She was transfixed, speechless, so she barely flinched as Jose walked over to her and wiped his hands on her apron. "Let's add 987654321z to that list, shall we? The heinous crime of cleaning fecal matter from one's hands in a manner unsan-itary and perilous to the health of others!" He grinned at her (like a lunatic, she thought, freshly escaped over some Spanish asylum fence). "Hmmm, I'm not satisfied with that." He scrutinized the defiled wall. "Needs a bit of red, a bit of *passion*." He bent down, picked up a ripe tomato from where it had fallen during Mrs. Mackenzie's crazed dance with the dog. He liked the heft of it, the plumpness of it, the gentle give of its flesh. He spun and launched it, gazed contentedly as seeds and pulp blended with the shit on the white background. Satisfied, he began to walk away, when he was stopped by a hiss from behind him.

"Savage!" He turned to gaze at her. "Animal!" Mrs. Mackenzie fought for another pejorative, found it. *"European!"* He turned away again. "I'm phoning the By-law Officer. I'm reporting your infractions."

"Ask me if I care," Jose tossed back over his shoulder as he disappeared through the hedge. And he meant it, he really didn't care any longer. Bylaws be damned, he was about to reclaim his life. That resolution was what further exacerbated the conflict and brought about its inevitable conclusion.

• • •

OFFICER BELL SIGHED as he got out of his car and watched Mrs. Mackenzie beetle across the lawn towards him. He adjusted his gun, then his sunglasses, reached into the glove box to bring out his digital camera and palmtop notebook. He hated these disputes between neighbours. He was an Enforcement Officer, not a Resolutions Dispute Facilitator. He liked the Bylaws, their precision. He liked catching people breaking them and punishing the wrongdoers. That was clean, clear, rewarding. He slept well those nights when he'd registered precise convictions. He disliked these personal feuds, my word against your word, he did it first, no he did, I witnessed this, she's a liar, I am not, blah, blah, blah. Give him the Bylaws, the flagrant infractions, the punishment unequivocally stated and meted out. Black and white. No grey.

The grey Mrs. Mackenzie, the complainant, was in his face, frantic. Her arms were windmilling and she was talking so rapidly and loudly he couldn't understand most of it. "Please, slow down; let me record this." He punched a key and turned on his notebook. " Now who did what?"

"That hateful Spaniard," and she pointed out Jose's house.

Officer Bell raised a finger. "Ma'am, I have to warn you that derogatory racial references are a breach of 323a," and he clicked a button on the notebook.

Mrs. Mackenzie licked her lips nervously. She didn't like the direction this was heading. "You've got it wrong, Officer, He's the Bylaw breaker, not me," and she began reciting a long litany of Jose's crimes against humanity.

"Any proof of these accusations, ma'am?"

"You want proof? Look at this ankle." She held her leg out for Officer bell to take a picture of with his digital camera. The puncture wounds looked raw and angry.

"No stockings on ma'am?"

"I had, I took them off after the beast attacked me. The one was all shredded…" her voice trailed off as she noticed the officer taking copious notes. "You aren't citing me for 617b, are you, Officer, it's just that I… I mean, all my other stockings are on the line drying and…"

He cut her off. He was growing impatient. "You seem to know these laws inside and out, Mrs. Mackenzie. You should therefore realize that 617a prohibits all men over the age of 75 from removing shirts in public and b states that all women over 75 must wear opaque stockings in public. It's a taste thing, a beautification measure if you will. How old are you?"

He had very blue eyes, icy blue, that chilled her so she could barely respond. "S-S—Seventy -seven."

"Noted," and he registered something else in the palmtop.

Mrs Mackenzie was beginning to think that perhaps this hadn't been the best idea after all. With considerably less enthusiasm she led the officer around to the back yard, where she showed him the shit- and tomato-spackled wall. Dutifully, he photographed the scene from several angles and keyed in the information. As he was about to leave the yard, he noticed the tomatoes. He looked cooly at her. "Are you aware that those tomatoes are staked?" His voice made "staked" sound like "tortured." "You are aware that new Agricultural Bylaw 62f forbids you to stake tomato vines? It's been proven that physically plants suffer from being tied up; even been conjectured that they have self-esteem, not as complex as humans', of course, but that our preventing them from spreading naturally and as they please may actually traumatize them."

"I've missed the Horticulture Club meetings this year…illness…my husband…I didn't know…" She felt lost, as if she had entered an unfamiliar house, one that contained more rooms than she had possibly imagined from outside and one that appeared to have no exits.

"Mrs. Mackenzie, as you are well aware, ignorance of the law is no excuse."

"Please," she said, "please, I'm not the criminal here, he is." With one hand she grabbed a handful of Officer Bell's uniform to get his attention, with the other she pointed to the Libertad house.

He curtly unhooked her claw from his previously crisp white shirt. He was fast losing patience with this annoying woman. "Mrs Mackenzie, 1602b specifically prevents physical contact between

Enforcement Officers and the general public. That is four infractions in five minutes." He entered the code.

Mrs. Mackenzie froze. Four infractions! A fifth and....well, she didn't want to contemplate the result of a fifth. This was all going horribly awry. She was the wronged individual here and yet she was on the verge of Penalty.

Just when she feared that her next inadvertent move might be the straw to break Officer Bell's back, Jose Libertad entered stage left and the officer's attention shifted. Because Jose was smoking, openly, brazenly puffing on an obscenely big, hand rolled cigarette.

"Sir, are you aware of By-laws 542a and 542c governing the importation and consumption of tobacco?"

"I am indeed, Officer." Jose's face was a mixture of defiance and serenity. He carried the look of the oppressed for whom the weight of subjugation has finally become an ounce too heavy, and who has finally decided to face the oppressor, and screw the consequences. Bell logged the two infractions. This was becoming more black and white all the time. When he looked up after completing this task he noticed, for the first time, the unleashed and unmuzzled Pepe at Jose's heels.

"And are you aware...?"

Jose cut him off, "Indeed I am," flagrantly leaning down and patting the free-range dog on the head. Officer Bell dutifully recorded numbers three and four.

"Mr. Libertad, I should warn you..." but once again Jose silenced him, this time with a kamikaze look as he stepped towards Mrs. Mackenzie, sucked deeply on his cigarette and blew the contents of his lungs into her sputtering face, completely fracturing By-law 542f. Then he stepped back and smiled lazily and knowingly, which is when he died, as Officer Bell smoothly unholstered his pistol and put four shots into Jose Libertad's big heart. "Unfortunately, that's five, sir, and the Penalty for five is termination," Officer Bell said to the body of Jose, around which scrabbled Pepe, freaked by the noise of the pistol and the smell of blood.

Mrs. Mackenzie looked sourly down on Jose, them strode swiftly forward to deliver a savage boot to his head. "Good on you, " she spat at his body, her face red with victory. Pepe leapt at her but she repelled him with a solid kick any Scottish footballer would be proud of. Her ascendancy, however, was short-lived.

"And that's your fifth, lady: 512a, offering an indignity to a corpse," said Officer Bell, just before he looked into her hate-twisted face, from which the colour was draining as the stopcock of realization opened wide. He shot her once, cleanly, right between the eyes. She fell heavily with the stamp of irony embedded on her visage.

Officer Bell's attention turned to Pepe, who was ballistic. He was running in circles, pissing as he went and yapping maniacally, stopping now to lick at Jose's face, now to sink his teeth into Mrs. Mackenzie's arm. Bell knew what needed to be done. The dog was nuts, and loose, a major infringement of the Codes. He had one bullet left in his big Colt revolver, which he lifted and sighted at the little pooch, who suddenly stopped his frenzied circumnavigation of the bodies and stood quivering, looking plaintively up the barrel into Officer Bell's clear blue eyes.

The officer reflected for a moment, thinking fondly back to his boyhood visits to his grampa's farm, and the old man's tiny beagle, how they'd run together across the open fields. He eased the hammer back down, lowered the barrel and smoothly reholstered his weapon. "C'mere boy," he said to Pepe, who at first stood his ground, then cautiously approached the Officer's outstretched hand, which he sniffed and found to his liking. Bell returned to his patrol car, extracted a leash and muzzle, which Pepe allowed him to put on him. Bell led the dog to the car and opened the door. Pepe leapt up onto the front seat, put his feet up on the dash and excitedly yipped at the scenery as Officer Bell set off in the direction of Headquarters and piles of forms to complete, passing unknowingly as he did Florence, who was blissfully returning home from her seminar and considering the merits of the recent linen/rayon blend, and of divorce from her increasingly troubling husband.

The Enforcement Officer was happy. It had all worked out cleanly. True, he could have served the Penalty on the dog but there were times when the Bylaws needed to be tempered with reason and mercy, right? He squared his shoulders and raised his chin. He was confident that he had made the right decision. As was Pepe, whose tail was wagging furiously at the bright future unwinding on the other side of the windshield. And who was wondering how he might convey to his new master that he badly needed to take a dump.

Anne Campbell

Pumpin' Gas

THE THING ABOUT being paranoid is it takes a lot of time. They say you just gotta extra keen mind and a nose for a situation but for the person who's got it it just plain takes a lot of time. You got to keep keeping everything straight. Like you suspect somebody doesn't want to see you. You got to keep that separate from the people who really don't want to see you. It takes a lot of thinking and naturally you can't tell anybody about all the time you put into it because nobody wants to hang around with somebody you thinks people don't want to hang around them. Get my drift? It's a bummer and also boring. See, if you get a refusal or somebody is busy or they say they can't see you, you have to have a talk with yourself. Say: well that's OK they're busy or that's OK they want to see somebody else. You have to de-flect the notion—like diggin' deep to get the puck out of your end of the ice. The people I envy are those guys who think everybody is crazy about them, and the ones that think everybody hates them. It's simple for them. I mean they believe what they think. It's hard to keep what you feel separate from the ideas in your head about why you feel that way. Like this guy keeps comin' in here to the station for gas—says he's a poet. So what does he tell me for? He says there's this other guy who don't like him much so when he sends a poem out to him it don't get published. Me, if that happened—which it wouldn't because I would-n't write a poem, or send it if I did—I'd probably think somebody did-n't like me too. But I'd have to think about it and reason it out and then when I still felt lousy because somebody didn't like something I made, I'd likely figure out there wasn't any way this guy knew me so my feeling lousy about it and thinking the guy didn't like me would be the paranoia again. See what I mean. A lot of time goes into sorting it all out and no thanks anyway because you can't write and tell some guy who doesn't know you that you figured out he doesn't hate you I mean he's think you were crazy. It takes a lot of time and for what. I don't know. I admit I like to keep things straight. Not get how I feel inside all mixed up with how I think a totally different person feels. Ahh…I guess I got the time, between pumpin'gas and fixin' flats. It ain't so bad, I guess, thinking it out if you got the time.

Shannon Cowan

Shortages

IT WAS A YEAR measured by scarcity, by the layering on of sweaters, by long dips in cool water when summer finally came around. Tempers seemed pegged to the price of gas, boiling inside transport cabs and the dingy service station office where Thomas worked after hours, plunging oily dipsticks into engines, making change from a tattered money belt. There was a nebulous discomfort in the humidity, a disquietude and lack of generosity that comes with too many people wanting what is short in supply. Thomas was in his final year of high school; he had just spent his last fifteen years disappointing twenty-seven consecutive teachers who mistook his high IQ for evidence that he cared. He was sheepish, aloof, with a blur of peach fuzz eroding the softness of his upper lip, habitually clad in a hooded sweatshirt that read *Keep on Truckin'*.

The building that ruled his life was located in the old part of town, at the end of a shaded street rimmed with sugar maples. The high school had the aging, shabby look of architecture that was once in style, but had passed quickly out of vogue when its engineers discovered the impracticality of gravel and tar roofs. Its squat windows leaked a wash of pale light onto speckled floors and walls insulated with asbestos. Ponds of water covered the low-pitched ball fields in a seasonal tide of dirt.

During the year in question, Thomas spent his lunch hours in the high school cafeteria, flipping the pages of novels with moistened fingertips, or dealing out cards to an arrangement of malcontents who sat at the wooden tables wringing their angst through games of *Asshole* or *Up and Down the River*. He didn't consider these boys his friends, but rather inmates sharing a surliness, a communal despair that they might never grow up, get out, be free. They waited for parole with an impatience that bored and frustrated them into strange displays of individuality, growing their hair into shaggy manes or painting their boots with political slogans done cursively in liquid paper. Some considered themselves philosophers trapped in teenaged bodies, although Thomas wasn't one of them. After a game of cards, Stewart of the black trench coats and the fingernails sharpened to points, inevitably leaned back in his chair and summed everything up. "One more peeling off the potato of life," he would say.

Their collective goal, although unspoken, was to preserve their sanity by doing whatever it took. In Thomas' case, this was as little as possible. He did not set out to be a slacker. He had a vague memory of enjoying the first few days of kindergarten, of painstakingly gluing hard yellow pasta to a mat of construction paper in a circular configuration. (His mother kept this early success tacked to the wall of her sewing room.) His parents had never owned a television, so Thomas had poured his considerable energy into novels, atlases, news weeklies, his father's collection of *National Geographics* stacked into musty towers on basement shelves. Somewhere between kindergarten and the beginning of high school, his curiosity waned, redirected itself, became an affliction. He didn't know how this had happened.

One of his last attempts to apply himself came not long into the school year, September or October. Thomas was sitting in Social Studies considering a wart on his thumb. Smoke from piles of burning leaves wafted through the windows, blurring the air with a haze of grey that reminded Thomas of a childhood visit to Niagara Falls. He had been up much of the previous night, fuelled by mugs of coffee and a fleeting, half-assed desire to participate. Now his eyes drooped; his gums itched with nervousness.

His teacher made silent rounds through the desks, checking for homework with the tick of his pencil against an aluminium clipboard. Already Thomas was drifting. Still, some small part of him wanted to see if he could pull something off.

"And Thomas?" his teacher said, raising a quizzical eyebrow. He was tall and friendly, avid with the cheerful innocence of the yet-to-be disappointed. "Are you ready to share your project with the class?"

Thomas knocked his knees against his desk. He had forgotten. Of course he had forgotten. He had been knee deep in Italo Calvino, imagining invisible cities stretching out before him like the frigging world map.

"Uh," Thomas said. "All right."

He walked tentatively to the blackboard and launched into an

idea that had struck him last night, and not, as his teacher expected, weeks ago when he'd been given the assignment. "Over the past
little while," he said with conviction, "I've been conducting a psy-
chology experiment with you as my subjects. I've been observing
you daily, doing tests to see how you would respond to certain
stimuli." He went on to tell them, the bored and drooping faces of
his Social Studies mates, that he now had his results. He waved a
piece of paper shamelessly in front of them all.

The piece of paper, Thomas noted, contained statistics that proved
his hypothesis, a convoluted behavioural observation patched
together at five o'clock in the morning. He had used rigorous
processes, empirical reasoning. He had made the whole thing up.

The performance mortified Thomas, and he walked away from the
blackboard clutching a piece of chalk. He felt giddy and exhausted,
weak with obvious transparency. His teacher gave him an A+.

"What do you figure," he said later to Stewart in the cafeteria.
"That we're doing here again?"

"Passing time," Stewart said. "Before we go out a make a mess of
things, like everyone else."

THOMAS' TOWN WAS located at the junction between two highways,
tucked into a scenic valley landmarked with aging barns, private ski
clubs, fields of cornstalks and leftover pumpkins, a Cistercian abbey.
Not far away, Lake Ontario glistened under a smog-choked sky, slug-
gish with enough mercury to develop photographs.

Joe's Gas sat near the centre of town, a lone service station dou-
bling as a bus depot. On Fridays and Saturdays, Thomas worked the
late shift, walking past grocery stores and a flapjacks restaurant from
his house by the river. Though they never got angry with Thomas,
his parents had insisted he limit his hours to the weekend in a final
show of discipline.

There were many reasons Thomas preferred the late shift: he did
not have to confront his bedroom in the dark, the orange bedspread
and a faux nautical headboard that made him feel as if he was riding steerage; he did not have to creep past the entreating eyes of
his mother, her face, tilted up momentarily from *I'm OK, You're OK*,
awash with concern for his well-being (and later, listen to the timid
rapping of that same mother's knuckles, after she arrived outside his

door, hesitated on the shag rug, before finally determining to offer him a mug of Horlicks); he did not have to look down the long dark tunnel of his future, advancing with the tick of his bedside clock, the swish of curtains drawn across an open window, moving over him like a slow but inevitable weather pattern that he must take pains to predict.

Ever since he could remember, Thomas had been a night owl, staying awake until dawn, sleepwalking through most of the day. On weekends especially, when he had the chance to sleep in, Thomas lingered in bed until two, cocooned in the smell of his covers (fabric softener, iron starch), inhaling his own damp sweat. Working the late shift, Thomas served truckers and long distance salesmen, men who opened up their trunks to show him vacuum cleaners and superior disinfectants. He listened to discussions about power suction or the presumptuousness of dirt, and then he filled their tanks, or he used to, before the price increases. Since then, no one had been in the mood to chat.

The first time he ran into Wayne Ashcroft at the gas station, Thomas was making his way into the parking lot. Puddles of oil glistened on pavement, surrounding the pumps between wads of flattened chewing gum. A Greyhound bus idled as passengers stretched and waited for the key to the bathroom. Thomas nodded to the bus driver as he approached the station. He heard Joe's voice echoing over the pumps.

"It's not that I don't need help," Joe said. "It's that I can't afford to take anyone on. I'm strapped as it is."

There was a pause and Thomas imagined Joe, a balding man in mechanical scrubs, studying his blackened fingernails. He knew from the papers that Joe was one of a few struggling independents not yet absorbed by the Standard Oil Company of New Jersey, or by Texaco, Exxon, and Shell. Joe was all by himself, and that was something Thomas understood.

A younger voice said in reply: "I'm trained."

"Look," Joe said. "I'm sorry. I really am. But I can't help you. Come back in a few months, maybe six. Maybe things'll be different."

Thomas heard a restless shuffle and he saw Wayne Ashcroft emerge from the station. A look of anger worked at his face. He muttered something that sounded like kiss my long johns, but

Thomas knew it was much more obscene, because everything that came out of Wayne's mouth was obscene, and because he followed the curse by kicking over a row of bicycles. The resulting heap was a tangle of metal.

Thomas knew Wayne. Usually he stood at the end of the blue hall by the automotive shop, smoking cigarettes down to their filters and taking courses with names like Gas Station Attendant. *The Dead End,* everyone called the blue hall. Thomas tried not to think about the implications.

At school Wayne wore year round heavy boots and a look of permanent indignation. He fixed up cars and broken down television sets and sold the results for beer. Before the principal redirected him to remedial English, Wayne sat behind Thomas in Language Arts, creaking his chair and carving *Bat Out of Hell* into the surface of his desk with a penknife. He raised his hand only once all year, when their teacher was giving a dissertation on the use of iambic pentameter.

"What are we going to use this for in life?" he wanted to know.

The teacher scoffed at Wayne's question and launched into a soliloquy.

Thomas remembered this moment as he watched Wayne curse the bicycles. Ever since then he had respected Wayne, though he still avoided him as much as possible.

"What are you looking at?" Wayne said to Thomas.

Thomas did an about face and headed into the station.

WORKING AT JOE'S GAS was not Thomas' ideal. He did not see himself, somewhere down the road, purchasing a station of his very own, going through the motions of pump, oil check, squeegee, end of pump, sales receipt, over and over until the dawn of his retirement. He did not see himself doing much of anything. He did consider briefly the look on Wayne Ashcroft's as he came out of the station and cursed. It was a look that told Thomas there was anger in the world, however misguided and strange, and that some of that anger might one day be directed at him.

As the energy crisis heated up in different parts of the world, Thomas' own energy sputtered and died. When he wasn't avoiding work at school, he was avoiding school at work. The rest of the time he was avoiding his parents. With his father, avoidance was not difficult. The man commuted one hundred miles to a sprawling suburb on the edge of the city where he spent long hours in a cubicle designing bus shelters. By the time he had navigated the freeways, the bypasses, the ten car pile-ups, and speeding traps back to his house on the river, Thomas was usually asleep or pretending to be, absorbed in the unrequited yearnings of his body. His mother was more difficult: she worked five days a week as the district nutritionist. Lately she had been serving him casseroles for dinner, mixtures of unrecognizable ingredients ground up and layered together. He suspected her of slipping him vitamins.

And then there were the ambushes. He knew from past conversations with both his parents that his lack of ambition wearied them. They were at the end of their conjoined rope. Soon they would seek help. When Thomas received the summons to the principal's office, he was not surprised.

"Thomas," said Mr. Higgins, as Thomas entered his office and slipped into a chair.

Higgins was a large man who came to his principalship after a career as a quarterback with the Ottawa Roughriders. His red face was flecked with veins. He peered out over a hefty chest that strained at his shirt buttons and spread the wings of his lapels. He eyed Thomas with a raised eyebrow before drumming his fingers on the desk. "So," he said. "We meet again."

Thomas smiled weakly.

"You must know why you're here. I don't need to tell you. You're failing math. You're failing English. Is there any reason for that?"

"Ambition is the last refuge of failure," Thomas offered. "Oscar Wilde."

"I see," Higgins said. "Just as I thought. There's no reason whatsoever." He leaned back in his chair and folded his hands over his head, peering beyond Thomas at the wall. "You will have to enlighten me Thomas. You are a bright boy. You come from a good home. I've met your parents. I know your mother. They seem like reasonable people."

"They are," Thomas said with a sense of impending judgement.

"Then why," Higgins said, focussing on Thomas. "Do you continually disappoint them? Why do you keep up this charade? Is it to make a fool of us all? Or maybe of yourself, is that it?"

Thomas said nothing. He recognized a rhetorical question when he heard one.

Higgins grunted and lifted a paper off his desk. He examined it briefly before returning his attention to Thomas. "I see you entered the Math contest."

"It was mandatory."

"I know it was mandatory," Higgins snapped. "I'm the principal, goddammit, not the secretary." He paused for a moment before recomposing himself. "I just received the results. Would you like to know how you did?"

"Not especially," Thomas said.

"Well I'm going to tell you," Higgins said. "You came first. You placed first in the province, out of all the students in your grade. You won the gold medal." He paused for effect. "Yet you are failing Algebra." He looked at Thomas for explanation. Thomas didn't have one.

"It was a general knowledge quiz," Thomas ventured. "It wasn't based on studying."

Higgins snorted and deposited the results in the waste paper basket. He fidgeted with his pen. "I have one question to ask you, and I want you to answer it honestly, no punches. None of your clever deceptions or sharp wit." He waited for Thomas to nod. "Why," he said. "Are you here?"

Thomas looked at his lap and shuddered. Did Higgins mean 'here' as in the building or 'here' as in the universe? Did he want Thomas to tell him the meaning of life? Either way, he didn't know how to answer the question: it wasn't something he'd spent much time considering. "Because I have no choice," he said eventually.

"That's what I thought," said Mr. Higgins. He stood up and offered his hand in a brisk gesture that unnerved Thomas. "From now on we are wasting no more time. No more conferences. No more pesky detentions. From now it's hands off. We will leave you alone. You will go about your business, and no doubt we will all be disappointed. But sometimes," he added with a look of remorse. 'That's the way life goes."

THOMAS AGREED WITH Mr. Higgins assessment. He'd heard it all before: that embittered sound of blighted hope—half resignation, half resentment. If only he applied himself, his Algebra teacher had echoed, hours before, when Thomas neglected to turn in his paper and nearly failed the term. If only he gave a damn.

Thomas did give a damn, but the things he cared about came and went as randomly as indigestion. He cared, for instance, that he would no longer be subjected to tests, the sort involving ink spots and symbolically shaped pieces of wood. He cared that he would never again be pulled from regular classes by the school board and forced into enrichment. No more afternoons spent in the Resource Room, a glorified closet lined with glass beakers and punctured vinyl basketballs, crammed in next to girls with yarn in their hair and a boy with a glass eye. No more calligraphy (he smudged everything, he was left-handed) or shouting out the solutions to mathematical riddles.

Even from the beginning, Thomas could tell that he was missing something: a vitamin, a soul. Other children were energetic, competitive, flashing their orthodontic smiles at the teacher, raising their evenly nibbled fingernails at the crack of the morning bell. They cared. They cared. Thomas didn't understand. He stepped from the principal's office into the waiting room, shouldering his school bag like a satchel of bones. The secretary flashed him a look of compassion, reminding him of his mother and the conversation that would ensue when he eventually went home.

In the corner, beneath a framed reproduction of Elizabeth II, another boy struck a match and held it briefly to a hand-rolled cigarette. Thomas recognized Wayne Ashcroft beneath a dirt-stained baseball cap.

"Mr. Ashcroft," the secretary said with barely concealed contempt. "You know very well you can't smoke in here. Put that out at once."

Wayne blew smoke through his nostrils, focussing a wry smile on Thomas. One. Two. "Excuse me. For living," he said, extinguishing the cigarette onto the upholstery.

BY SUMMER THE energy crisis was in full swing. Thomas read the ministrations of federal politicians, the protests of local independents against bloodsucking conglomerates. He shivered and then sweated as his mother set the thermostat and the ceiling fans according to guidelines on national public radio.

At work tempers were rising. People did not like deprivation.

They did not like lining up. Thomas cleaned bugs and grime off windshields, ignoring the cold stares of drivers through the glass. He tried to project innocence.

"We will not be getting ice cream," he heard one mother snap at her children who were whining in the back seat. "We just spent all our money on gas."

As the final weeks of the school year ticked away, Thomas wondered about his own carelessness. Did he really want to fail? Is that what he was doing? He consulted Stewart in the cafeteria.

"You don't give a shit," Stewart pronounced. "There's nothing wrong with that. It's not like we're cracking code here. Everything we learn has already been discovered."

Thomas studied the line up of boys at his table hunching over bagged parcels of roast beef sandwiches and miniature urns of pudding. Most of them were pink-faced, speckled with dermatological conditions or uneven swaths of stubble. "Easy for you to say. You're going to pass."

"That's because I study," Stewart said, without malice. And it was true. Stewart completed his assignments; he didn't make excuses. He plodded through papers on the Canadian Constitution and Hamlet's Oedipal complex with something approaching interest. He kept his despair under control. "It's not that you can't do the work. It's that you won't. There's a difference between stupidity and laziness." He paused to pull on his drink-n-box. "Enter exhibit 'A'."

Thomas followed Stewart's glance to the far end of the cafeteria where a group of featureless students clothed in bulky jackets and unlaced boots were making their way towards an empty table.

"Wayne Ashcroft et al," Stewart said in a low voice. "Has been in his final year for how long? Soon he'll be eligible for a pension. That, my friend, is not laziness alone."

Thomas watched as Wayne selected a chair and anchored himself to its moulded plastic surface.

"Of course, he's handicapped. He has a primate for a father."

Thomas said nothing. He knew this much about Wayne's father: he was a salesman with a bad temper who lived in a shingled house with his wife and son. During hunting season he donned a checked mackinaw and drove north where he shot a deer, strapped it to the front of his car, and then drove back to town the long way displaying the carcass like a hood ornament. Thomas had twice seen his wife in the butcher's running her hands over the stacked flanks of packaged meat, a yellow bruise spreading from beneath her sunglasses.

"It's amazing that he's here at all," Stewart said. "And not home prying the crankcase off a stolen engine block. Did you ever wonder why they call them monkey wrenches?"

"Hey," Thomas said, giving Stewart a sharp look.

"Right," Stewart said. "I forgot. No service station jokes." He returned his attention to his French fries, congealing now in a pool of gravy. A few tables away, in a black T-shirt and blue jeans, Wayne Ashcroft hooted loudly.

THOMAS TRIED TO care about his future, but his efforts did not manifest themselves in anything like a reversal. He moved slowly through the daytimes, the evenings, sitting quietly at the family dinner table while his mother trucked out stories over mashed potatoes and tuna fish casserole.

"Remember how much you used to entertain?" she said. "You were a regular Abbot and Costello."

Thomas did remember, vaguely, the antics his mother talked about. Back when he was a freckled, apple-cheeked child in flannel panamas and a Bay City Rollers haircut, he frolicked in the living room, swooping and prancing for guests who urged him on with polite guffaws and sips of virgin eggnog. He had boundless energy, unlimited brains. His future was bright indeed.

"You were so happy," his mother added. "Such a happy little boy."

Thomas remembered happiness. He remembered feeling normal. Sometimes he still felt normal, but then he had a conversation like this one.

"I just worry about you," his mother went on. "You seem so singular."

There it was again: his mother believed everything would be different if only he had a girlfriend. His heart was chipped; his ducts were blocked. He picked at his Royal Chinette dinner plate, tasting the mix of salt and hairspray and cherry flavoured lip-gloss that would greet him when he first placed his tongue on any number of the female places he imagined nightly. It wasn't as if he'd been saving up.

Still, he knew his mother wasn't trying to annoy him. She cared, and that made matters worse. Affection immobilized him, particularly the sincere adhesive sort that oozed from his parents like a force field in a comic book. It made him want to hide.

"I love you Thomas," his mother said. "Of course you know that."

"Yep," said Thomas, choking back a Brussels sprout.

When guilt did get the better of him, he decided to divert himself.

"Your final project of the year," his English teacher said, one morning in June. They were back at school after the weekend. Thomas was feeling desperate.

"A comparison of three novels," the teacher continued. "I want thorough reading. I want original ideas. I want," he stopped and surveyed at them all. "Your absolute best."

The class groaned.

"I'm sure you will all find this fascinating. I know I did when my teacher forced me to do it, several years ago. Though perhaps only in retrospect."

Another groan.

"In any case, I am expecting success. Your only job is to make it happen."

DOING THE READING was not a problem. Thomas had already cracked the spines of several hundred books while attending various family gatherings and boring assemblies. Seated on couches, hard-backed wooden chairs, a porch glider, and a tobacco-scented chintz ottoman, he ploughed through words that he didn't understand, situations that made no sense, just so he wouldn't have to play another round of *The Game of Life* with his cousins.

"My he's studious," his aunt had said, on more than one occasion.

"Yes," his mother had answered. "So I see."

Reading for school was different. The books were thin and dog-eared, printed on yellowing paper. Some of the pages had fingerprints daubed across important scenes; others had obscene pencilled-in footnotes decrying the state of a teacher's earwax. The subject matter was prairie writing, and all of them were bleak with hopelessness, with depression-era fortitude. Thomas pictured rotting farmhouses, locust plagues, combine tracks petrified in driveway mud; he read about livestock frozen in freak whiteouts and wells slowly poisoned with dust. He wondered: why didn't they all just kill themselves?

He found himself wandering, picking up science fiction books, cleaning underneath his bed. He even helped his mother hull a vat of strawberries, which made her ruffle his head affectionately and kiss him on the cheek. Anything was better than work.

Was this the best he could do? He wondered silently to himself, as the days advanced and he made less and less effort. Was this the sum of his fate? As usual his assignment was half the length it should have been, a loose rambling of poorly formulated arguments and condescending psychobabble. He hadn't allowed himself time enough for more. His teacher gave him a passing grade, but it wasn't enough.

"Congratulations," Mr. Higgins said when Thomas was back in his office. "You failed your final year of high school. By two percent."

Thomas cringed. His long downhill slide had ended. He was a loser, a numbskull. He was a Wayne Ashcroft.

"We have a road before us," Mr. Higgins continued. "A road with many challenges."

Thomas tried to concentrate on Higgins' voice, rising over the whir of summer lawn mowers, but somehow he wandered off, travelled to the inner reaches of his brain where fifteen years of academic lint stewed in cerebral fluid: *Agricolo, agricolas, agricolat. The square of the hypotenuse equals the sum of the squares of the other two sides. Tomorrow and tomorrow and tomorrow. To the last syllable of recorded time.* He felt strangely calm.

"I should fail you," Higgins went on. "Because you've done nothing all year but avoid work." He banged his desk with his fist as if to emphasize his point. "But I refuse."

Thomas snapped to attention. "Excuse me?" he said, back from beyond. He wasn't hearing right.

Higgins gave him a long look. "I know your game, and I refuse to participate. I refuse to assist you with the destruction of your life."

Thomas stared at his high school principal, searching his face for a clue, a shred of irony or cruel humour. There wasn't any. The man was serious.

"Go out there and make something of yourself," said Mr. Higgins, clutching his desk with beefy fingers. "And don't ever say nobody did you a favour."

OUTSIDE THE HIGH school Stewart waited for Thomas.

"So," he said. "Are you a free man?"

Thomas kicked his boots into the ground, his mind still blurring with the logic of his narrow escape. What was Higgins thinking, letting him walk like that? He said so himself that Thomas had proven nothing but avoidance. "Seems that way," he said.

"Looks like you're one of the lucky ones." Stewart said, motioning across the green. On the other side of the turnabout, Thomas saw Wayne dragging on a cigarette, his baseball cap low over his eyes. The same group of friends lingered around him, snapping the tabs off pop cans and flicking ash into the grass. "Word has it he'll be back for another try."

Thomas stared at the school, examining bricks and mortar, surveying a series of stacks and chimneys that protruded from the gravel and tar roof. He glanced at a garden where cheery tulips proclaimed *Welcome to your Future!* in five jubilant colours, trying to imagine what he would do with his life now that he was free. He had no plans whatsoever.

"What's eating you?" asked Stewart.

"Nothing," Thomas said. In reality, something was bothering him. He just didn't know what to make of it.

WHATEVER WAS EATING Thomas grew inside him like a slice of anger. By the time he was back at work, serving customers who were beginning to gather for the late night bus, the feeling had worked away at his insides so that his stomach growled with indignation. Up until that moment, Thomas had tolerated his job, the irate drivers, the black tar that softened on hot summer days and stuck to the bottoms of his shoes. He had put up with long shifts and clothes stained with engine oil, because the job was another diversion that took his mind off school. Standing in the station, beneath a sign for Joe's Gas that lit up the night like an all-dressed hamburger—red, yellow, and green—Thomas realized he had come to loathe his job. But now the job was all he had.

"Can I help you?" he said to the next customer while he fiddled with his receipt book.

"Two tickets to Toronto," a voice said.

Thomas looked up to see Wayne Ashcroft standing with his legs apart. His jacket was torn open at the neck; his left eye was swollen into a purple bruise. He fingered a number of small bills and passed them across the counter.

"Uh," said Thomas, counting the money. "The rate went up with the price of gas. I'll need another twenty."

Wayne looked at Thomas and didn't move. A cut on his lower lip had dried to a brown smudge.

"Can we get a move on," said a man behind Wayne. "I got a long ride ahead."

"Right with you," Thomas said. He smiled sheepishly at Wayne and served the man, punching numbers into the cash register. A strange nervousness disabled his fingers. He had to do the whole thing twice. When he was finished, a woman stepped inside. Thomas recognized Mrs. Ashcroft.

"Wayne?" she said hoarsely, clutching the handle of a duffel bag. "Is there a problem?" She wore sunglasses and a toque drawn down to her eyebrows. She took measured steps towards the counter.

"Just a minute," Wayne said to Thomas. He ushered his mother through the racks of Archie comics and low-grade hot wheels porn tucked into plastic sleeves and hidden behind the crosswords.

"I've got something," he said when he was back at the counter. He riffled in his pocket and took out a photograph, a black and white portrait of someone in a heavy metal band. From where Thomas stood, he could make out muscles, dark make-up, stainless steel metal studs. Across the photo a message was scrawled in slanting letters: *For Wayne, stay cool.* There was an unreadable signature. "I'll give you this for the difference," Wayne said.

Thomas hesitated, his chest constricting. Wayne watched him warily from his good eye. The photo lay between them on the counter, shiny in the station lights.

"Last call," the bus driver hollered into the station. "Everyone on board."

Thomas fiddled with the photograph. The feeling that had been bothering him flashed now in the frontal lobes of his brain: Wayne failed, but Thomas passed. Thomas passed. "O.K," he said to Wayne, filling out the tickets and putting the photo into the cash register.

Wayne eyeballed Thomas. "One more thing," he said.

"Yeah?" Thomas fidgeted.

"Anybody comes along looking for me, you didn't see me here."

Thomas nodded, feigning a slow understanding. He didn't know what Wayne was talking about.

WHETHER OR NOT he understood Wayne, Thomas knew one thing: he had counted on failing, that much was true. He had counted on the long slow dive of his own neglect. Trying and doing poorly was worse than not trying at all, so he hadn't tried, ever. It was easier than figuring out what to do with his life. When Mervin Ashcroft arrived at the station, Thomas had just shut down the pumps and stood thinking beneath the station lights. He heard a car revving down Second Street. He stepped outside as it pulled into the lot.

"Fill it," Ashcroft said.

Thomas bent into the open window of a Lincoln Continental. "Hello Mr. Ashcroft," he said. "How are you this evening?"

"Cut the crap," Ashcroft said, lighting a cigarette with shaking hands. "I need a full tank and no funny business. I've got to be somewhere."

Thomas took a step back and made a show of yawning. He made some mental calculations. The pieces were coming together: Wayne's failure, his purple face. The woolly toque drawn across his mother's forehead. Escape by Greyhound. "I'm sorry to have to tell you this, but I filled you yesterday, remember? I can only give you ten dollars' worth. Those are the rules."

Mervin Ashcroft expelled smoke onto the tar-stained upholstery. "Don't fuck with me," he pointed at Thomas. "Just give me the gas."

Thomas took another step back and butted up against the pumps. Momentarily, he saw his life twisted in the grip of Mervin Ashcroft's hands. "I can give you ten dollars," he repeated calmly. "That's all I can do."

Ashcroft cursed and banged his fist on the dashboard. A garter belt suspended from his rear view mirror jumped in surprise. Within seconds he was outside the Lincoln, raging in the parking lot. He brandished a fist near Thomas' nose. "Turn on these pumps or I will flatten you like there's no tomorrow."

Thomas briefly considered the fist. He had a decision to make. He willed his brain to help him. "An education is an admirable thing," he muttered softly to Mervin Ashcroft. "Although it is common knowledge that nothing worth knowing can be taught. Oscar Wilde."

"What?" said Mr.Ashcroft.

"An education is an admirable thing—" Thomas began again.

The force of Ashcroft's fist sent Thomas sprawling against the pumps. There was the crack of an older man's fingers against a younger man's nose. There was blood on the pavement. In the instant before Thomas hit the ground, he saw a loose-leaf advertisement rising to his face, one that he had previously seen floating around the parking lot. *World Book Encyclopaedias: go out on a limb for learning.*

WHEN THOMAS CAME to he was looking into the face of an RCMP constable.

"You took quite a hit," the constable said. "A neighbour heard the ruckus and thought someone was trying to steal gas. She thought we'd better come out and have a look."

"Mr. Ashcroft?" Thomas said.

"Another car nabbed him for speeding. Seems he was in quite a hurry after leaving here. On his way to the city. He's cooling off in a cell."

Thomas got carefully to his feet and thanked the constable for helping him. Up in the sky the stars winked, reminding him of a constellation map he'd created once using a flashlight and a sheet of carbon paper. This was back in grade seven, when his love of learning still thrilled him, when he cared enough to go out on a limb. He made his way to the bathroom where he cleaned the dirt off his face and dabbed gingerly at his nose. It felt very much like a brick.

THE DAY OF his graduation, Thomas sat down in his high school cafeteria where rows of plastic chairs replaced the heavy wooden tables. He listened to the speeches of his classmates and teachers, the rounds of polite applause. He fiddled with the tassel on his mortarboard. When the time came, he walked across the stage and collected his piece of paper, sweating beneath his polyester gown in a pair of corduroy dress pants. His mother captured everything on film, in case Thomas should ever want to look back on his high school days and think fondly about his narrow escape. And from time to time, when he did, this is what he saw: Thomas in a chair, leaning into the valedictory address as though it would sweep him away. Thomas walking the narrow wooden floorboards of the stage, his gown caught between his legs like the pucker on curtain. His mother even captured his one and only handshake with Mr. Higgins, a tight squeeze that had briefly pinched the bones in his hand. Thomas had walked away from the stage feeling startled and relieved.

The final picture on the roll showed Thomas and Stewart climbing the chain-link fence behind the school grounds, their faces stretched into a mock joy and desperation. Thomas remembered this photograph most of all. For once in his life he had felt motivated to go somewhere, to get away. He was as curious as anyone to see where that might be.

Sylvia Adams

Thai-Dyed

Coming back to sobriety, a dark, leafless country
bracing for sub-zero depression,
I'm still dressed like a tourist
courted by Bangkok markets.
I'm sporting breezy caravan pants,
tie-dyed black swirling to white and a coral
soon laundered to pale orange.
It's the last week of October.
A Canadian accent comes up behind me:
"You look like you're ready for Hallowe'en!"
A friend avoids looking at me,
says older women don't dress
the way they used to.
What do you want, I want to say,
fortrel pant suits in olive drab,
black dresses from chin to ankle
and perhaps a return those underpants
in navy, fleece-lined cotton
that once armoured thighs and knees?

This country could use some colour culture shock,
something to whet the couturier's palette:
Memories of Far East Ramblings
or Touristus Seductibus.
Meanwhile – Colours Anonymous, maybe?
a number to call: *Help!*
I'm about to buy kelly-green stockings,
a bustière ablaze in purple sequins
and, yes! I confess I have nights when
I dream I'm Lana Turner
encased in a lipstick-red sweater
at a dime-store soda fountain,
waiting to be discovered.

And those Thailand market bargains
triumphantly borne through customs:
consigned to second hand stores
or cut down for children too young
to argue about their wardrobe
– or perhaps just old enough
to take pride in masquerades,

not fearing to interrupt winter,

shout colour down those dark hollows
where we doze,
jolt us awake

Sylvia Adams

Squiring a Squirrel to Burlington

My brother once drove a squirrel
from Dundas to Burlington.
It was planting time and my brother preferred
his perennials.
I could picture the catch of the day
rubbernecking in the passenger's seat
giving the royal wave to his friends,
thumbing his nose at the neighbourhood cats

thinking, I'm King of the World
– with a classic lack of originality.
(This was a squirrel who wasn't too swift,
exhausted from digging up bulbs.)

A friend of mine, an old hand at trapping,
bagged a gaggle of squirrels in a single day,
drove them out onto County Road Nine
where they partied 'til dawn, it never occurring
to any of them that the designated driver
had sold them a one-way trip.

But my brother's a softie. His chosen destination
offered more glitz than a ditch
at the forest's edge out back of beyond.
(Though in truth the party animals
had taken their fate in stride,
rearranging demographics
in their untapped housing project.)

The Dundas-Burlington trip is long enough
for captor and captive to bond;
and my brother, growing quite fond of his charge,
almost relented and took him home:
just a harmless herbivore yearning for
a bellyful of delphiniums!

Musing, my brother missed an insidious crunching
'til the steering wheel started to wobble,
came away in his hands.
A sheepish squirrel with a hangdog look
was more than my brother could bear –
the squirrel, who sat there picking his teeth,
missed salvation by a hair.

Jay Dolmage

Imposing Order II: Beaver Bulletin

Hello Parents:

W ELL, IT LOOKS like your son is a Beaver! I, Flying Chipmunk (a.k.a June Bergson), would like to take this opportunity to speak for the whole Beaver gang and welcome your child into the den! This is going to be a FUN year in scouting. As a matter of fact, this year is going to be an extra large fun with a side-order of fun. This Beaver Lodge is the most fun place in Windsor for your son to be on Thursday night. Believe it. But in order to help our program run as smoothly as the furry pelt of our favorite rodent, we need to have a few rules and regulations:

1. Our meetings start at 6:30 p.m PROMPTLY, and finish at 7:30. A good beaver is eager. But 5:30 is way too eager. This is the sort of eager that means your kid is just going to have to wait outside. And sometimes it's cold out there. Also, if you're the kind of parent that's always late, don't think that Beaver leaders don't have places to go at 7:30 on Thursday nights, because we do, and don't think that we won't go to these places, leaving your kid to wait by himself and learn some independence.

2. Each boy must be in full uniform. You can purchase these from Rainbow or Tic-Tac or Big Bear. Consider this a warning tail-smack on the pond that no uniform means not acceptable. We mean it. Kids that wear things like a jean jacket instead of a vest might be asked to go home and change or stay and clean things.

3. The first Thursday of every month is Dues Night. Dues are $20.00 per month. If dues aren't paid, we might have a financial situation like we did last year. Then kids might have to do without craft supplies and work for their drama badge all the time instead.

4. Good beavers get badges and different colors of fuzzy felt tails to

pin to the back of their hats. If you want to know how your kid is doing, look and see if he has a brown tail or a colorful one. If it's brown, he's probably not trying hard enough. Also, if you're kid is tucking his tail up in his hat to hide it, it's probably brown, and he's probably not trying hard enough. You can help him get Eager Beaver Industry Badges by doing the 'kits' which we will give you. This might be a lot of folding things or putting things together or in envelopes, but it is worth it when your kid has a sash full of badges and a colored tail. Want to help? Do the 'kits.' Not to be confused with another kind of 'kit'—a real baby beaver! We don't have those! Other special chances for getting badges are on Fruit Day, when kids go away with a bell and a bucket of fruit and come back with a bell and money. They should have a bath and a hair-cut before that day. The kids who sell the most fruit get a cheer and a fruit badge.

5. In our program, we follow the story "The Friendly Forest." The names of the beaver leaders have been changed to be the names of the characters in the story, so that the kids think the story is about us, when really it isn't. Don't tell your sons this. In the lodge, we go by the names Rainbow, Hawkeye, Tic-Tac, Big Bear, Jim-Bob and Flying Chipmunk—that's me. You can call us by our real names on the phone or away from the den, like at say Billy's Tavern or Arby's, but not at meetings or around the kids. It is a good idea to read the story, too, which can be purchased from us, so that you know what your kids are talking about when they say things about the Happy Trees, or sing the Sap Song, or try to scare their little sister with the story of the Haunted Stump. Your kids may say some things about Rusty and Bubbles. Just so you know, Rusty and Bubbles aren't leaders, they just hang out here some times and have no real parts in the story.

6. Some kids have bigger heads than other kids, so make sure the beaver hat fits the beaver head. Or else it will always fall off because it only fits on the very top part of his head. You can get the beaver hats in big sizes by ordering them through the mail. Some people have big heads. So what.

7. Some days, Beavers is going to be cancelled.

8. The Brownies have their meetings at the Public School too. But you should let your kids know that this year us beavers don't talk to brownies. This is the new policy. This is to avoid the problem of fistfights and what have you. Also, if your daughter is going to brownies while your son is going to beavers, make sure they both know that they can't talk and visit, even if one of them wants to go home. Crying is what the Lodge Closet is for, and girls aren't aloud in the Lodge Closet, they have their own Flower Closet. We know a lot of parents think family is important, and so do real natural Beavers. But we think family is less important than discipline sometimes.

9. In each Little Lodge, which is a small group of beavers, there are other rules. The kids all have different levels of powers. If your kid is called a Runt Kit, then he might be new to the Lodge or just not moving up very fast. If this is what's happening, please help your kid want to improve by reminding him how he's a Runt Kit, which is the bottom, which is for bottom-feeders at the bottom of the pond, which is dark and cold. If your kid is a Lodge Lord, you probably already knew about it because Lodge Lords don't keep it secret! The levels are for teaching kids how to be in charge or how not to be in charge.

10. If you get another letter from me or one of the other leaders about your son, you can rest assured that there's a problem. We communicate when we have problems. There is the wrong way of doing things, then there is the Beaver way of doing things, which is the FUN way. Your son needs to be prepared for this, because this is how it will be.

AND THOSE ARE the rules. But now, I want to take this chance to ask you, the parents, one big important question—is your kid a worker? If yes, then welcome to the den. We're always looking for good workers with normal behaviors. But before you send your kid away every week, make sure and ask yourself—is it fair to be sending your son to people other than your family to take care of him?

The beaver motto is 'share share share' but another important word is the word 'normal.' Ask yourself is your kid normal? Or can he be for an hour?

FINALLY, JUST SO you don't think I'm all business, I want to talk about some of the extra bonus fun we have planned. There will be one walk to the pizza place every second month. Real beavers go on trips outside of the den to around the pond for wood or maybe fish, snakes and other things to eat. We go for pizza! And the Arcade! Remember, kids who don't have quarters might not get to play the video games or the skee-ball and might feel left out and poorer than other kids. Which we won't be responsible for.

Also, each summer it's our special pleasure to do the overnight trip. This year, as usual, we'll go somewhere up North. Remember, kids aren't allowed in the Leader Tents and need to bring their own food. This is always a FUN FUN time for everyone who can come and pay the extra Dues for it! Beavers is not responsible for what goes on after flashlights-out, but kids should be encouraged to practice being quiet whatever they're doing.

Thanks for your time. I know that I speak for all of us leaders— Rainbow, Hawkeye, Tic-Tac, Big Bear, Jim, and me, Flying Chipmunk—when I say boy, are we eager to spend an hour with your son every Thursday. Hope your son is eager too, and prompt, and prepared, and normal, and has his dues, and is ready to work.

Yours Truly,
Flying Chipmunk

Hazel Jardine

Vacuum Fall-Out

T HERE WAS A fellow around the other day selling nuclear powered vacuum cleaners. I was in the middle of making buns and really didn't have time for him but it was hard to get his foot out of the door. So I let him in and he dragged his machine and a big black case upstairs to the living room. He crossed the carpet, looked alarmed and asked me if I'd heard anything. I said no, but he insisted he could hear the grit crunching in the carpet.

He opened everything out and began putting little piles of sand here and there. Then he started up the reactor and ran the vacuum nozzle up and down my arm. I began hoping my husband would soon be home. But he seemed to be only interested in sucking up my skin and having me agree it was sucked up all right.

He kept pulling white hankies out of a box and wrapping them around the filter. He'd vacuum and vacuum and keep showing me all the mess on the hanky. I was impressed, although I thought my carpet had a rather surprised look and I wondered if I'd ever get it settled down again. He was raving about the strength of the suction and I said I'd worry about anyone down the basement. Would they smash up into the ceiling when I ran it or would their hair just stand on end? He was not a humourous man and went on with his spiel about fluff balls and allergies.

I told him I was concerned about the nuclear energy part, how we're poisoning the globe and can't get rid of the wastes. He said it was a dangerous world we lived in, that we must take some risks. He said in 1000 years the wastes would be harmless. In fact, he seemed so alarmed that I might not buy one from him, that he ate a spoonful right there out of the canister. He said his machine actually ran on plutonium that emits no gamma rays. Said he carries a lump of it around in his pocket for good luck just wrapped up with paper. He liked to rub it and think about things.

I told him I really didn't need a vacuum , and he hadn't convinced me that it was safe. I didn't like the way my aloe vera plant was leaning over the stair well and going nobby on the ends. I finally said I had to get back to my baking and he muttered how I was one of those left wing people who think God didn't make plutonium so we shouldn't use it.

At the door he turned and I was surprised to see tears in his eyes. "Give me a break, lady," he said. "I'm working my way through college and haven't sold a nuclear vacuum for ten years." He said he'd throw in an irradiation kit and a year's supply of insecticides. I had to bang the door rather hard on his ankle several times before he finally left and went limping out to his van.

I felt kind of badly but, even in a province that's open for business, you just can't buy everything that comes knocking at your door.

Gina Rozon

For This, You Need a University Degree?

I ONCE OWNED a computer that would only work properly if I waved a metal tack hammer in front of it and issued verbal threats. I am not making this up. I know I won't find this troubleshooting solution in any tech manual ever written but it ought to be there. It worked every time. Well, almost every time. I had to be persistent. And patient.

So when I tried to learn the ins and outs of a new computer program and started to run into problems, I didn't give up. I persisted. Patiently. Well, patiently at first. At least for the first hour. Okay, the first half-hour. There's only so many times I can save a document and then discover the formatting is messed up. Then I start to think nasty thoughts about the unknown something running around inside the computer, taking bites out of my text and ENLARGING or reducing letters for no apparent reason.

If I were a paranoid type of person I would probably start to think that the program, or maybe even the computer, was out to get me. That it had a personality that took some sort of perverse pleasure out of tormenting the hand that feeds it (I do pay the electricity bill). I wouldn't be alone in thinking along these lines. Many people are convinced that the technology that plagues them is doing it on purpose.

I read of a recent poll that reveals that one in 10 Canadian workers attack photocopiers. Okay, a photocopier and a computer are two different pieces of technology but you get the idea. Why physically abuse the equipment unless you believe it has a brain buried deep inside it? A brain that is gloating as it chomps it's way through your hours of hard work – spitting out garbled text or shredded paper in response to your properly inserted instructions?

I'm beginning to think there may be more to my office machinery than meets the eye.

That poll I read suggests that photocopier rage is an issue for millions of Canadians. Not just a few. Millions. I am not making this up. The poll, conducted by Hewlett-Packard, indicates that office managers should seat university-educated employees as far from the photocopier as possible. This would be in an effort to limit their access to the equipment. Okay, I made that part up.

What the poll really said was that people with a university education are more likely to give in to their photocopier rage urges and kick or hit the machine. So it makes sense to keep them away from the photocopier, now doesn't it?

And if university educated people have determined that the technology is out to get us, who am I to argue?

Like the small percentage of office workers who say they have successfully restrained their urge to resort to physical violence, I turned to a book for the answer to my dilemma. I ordered in a massive tome written in a close approximation of sixteenth century Latin. It told me what I had already suspected. I was doing everything right.

Did you just hear that evil chuckle? I gave that old computer away years ago but I know I still have the tack hammer around here somewhere...

Bob Stamp

Disaster Services Officer

Alberta Municipal Affairs advertises
for a Disaster Services Officer
in the Careers section of today's newspaper:

Successful applicant will operate
under periods of prolonged stress,
with excellent interpersonal
and communication skills.

Perhaps I'll apply after this week's
litany of household disasters:

> water seeps through basement walls
> onto rumpus room carpeting

> fax machine garbles
> urgent data for tax preparer

> computer loses messages
> listing new e-mail addresses

> dishwasher goes on the fritz
> vacuum cleaner seizes up

I now claim vital experience operating
under periods of prolonged stress
although a few too many "god-damn-its"
(and several unprintable four-letter words)
compromise my interpersonal
and communication skills
so I'll never get the job.

Still, there's plenty to do at home:

> our black cat just barfed
> on the new two-hundred dollar mat
> and we're out of rug cleaner.

("Disaster Services Officer,"
Calgary *Herald*, April 20, 2002)

Cathy Jewison

Diamond Girl

"QUICK, CLAIRE! Here he comes!"

A salesclerk strolled out to join her co-worker bundling daisies at the counter of the florist shop in Yellowknife's downtown mall. The women watched a scrawny young man in jeans, a black bomber jacket and white sneakers wander past. He headed into the public washroom, a large backpack slung over his shoulder.

Work on the daisies slowed. A few minutes later, a businessman wearing a rumpled suit and white sneakers emerged from the men's room, one hand carrying a briefcase, the other smoothing his mustache. He strutted to the florist shop and attempted to lean on the counter. Peering through a low-hanging grey wig, he misjudged the distance – his elbow slipped and he pitched forward, almost smacking his chin on the counter top. His second attempt to strike a pose succeeded.

"Cheerio, love," he said in a well-practised English accent. "A perfect red rose – there's a good girl."

Claire smirked at her co-worker, who scuttled into the cooler. Claire's fingers arranged and re-arranged pieces of ribbon, while she stared at the man. He tried to make eye contact, but the over-powered glasses perched on his beaked nose caused her face to swim in the middle distance. He smiled and winked in her general direction.

"Your 'stache is slipping, Gerald," she said.

Gerald hiked the drooping corner of his false mustache into place. He glanced around.

"I don't think the enemy agents noticed," Claire said.

The other clerk returned and was about to wrap the rose. Gerald took it from her.

"I prefer it *au natural*," he said, trailing the blossom under the clerk's chin.

"What would Krystal say?" she asked.

"It's okay, babe. Everyone knows I'm out playing the field."

"Ya. Left field," Claire said. "And Krystal would be relieved to hear you'd transferred your affections elsewhere."

Gerald tossed his head in scorn. He retrieved his wig from the floor. The clerk gave him his change.

Slinking amongst the stumpy office towers and squat, middle-aged buildings of downtown Yellowknife, Gerald pulled at his wig and squinted through his glasses. He stopped to peer at the passing faces, lit by the sunshine of a fall morning. The denizens of Yellowknife seemed oblivious to his existence. As if. Despite his efforts, the eyes of any number of enemy forces could be trained on him. He removed a pen from his suit jacket, clicked a button and lifted it to his lips.

"Monday. Ten-hundred hours. Corner of 50 and 50. Code orange."

As Gerald replaced the pen, his fingers brushed a warm piece of metal. He smiled and pulled it out. Scratched and worn, it was his father's "James Bond" knife. Years earlier, eight-year-old Gerald had awoken to find it under his pillow, the very day his father had disappeared on his secret government mission. Gerald's father had often shown his son the wonders of the multi-blade knife: a saw for severing bonds; razor-sharp edges for dispatching your enemy to the next world; and, most importantly, a corkscrew for wining and dining the babes. If only his dad could see him now.

A pedestrian crashed into Gerald. He dropped the knife.

"Sorry buddy," the pedestrian said. "Didn't see you."

Gerald retrieved his keepsake, then watched the man disappear down the street. It was time to conclude his day's mission.

Moments later, Gerald arrived at the offices of the Borealis Diamond Mining Company, not far from where he'd started his trek almost an hour earlier. His impaired vision was no hindrance to finding his way – he was guided by the gleam of platinum hair and a pink V-neck sweater emanating from the reception desk at the far end of the lobby.

Krystal.

Her radiance was not the glow of midnight sun on a summer's eve; it was the winter glare of afternoon snow, a brilliance so sharp it could blind. She was currently using a nail file to attack one of her talons, and her molars to assault a wad of chewing gum. Gerald approached and laid the rose across the reception desk.

"Cheerio, love," he said.

Krystal stopped sawing and looked up.

"You're late. I missed coffee because of you."

"You're beautiful when you're angry, babe."

"The security company called forty-five minutes ago to say you'd left their office. Barry's been tearing his hair out."

Gerald patted his bulging briefcase. "Had to make sure no one was following. Special dispatches today."

"As if you'd know. Has it occurred to you that we don't need a courier, considering Wolverine Security is a block away, and one of their staff could run stuff over in two minutes? Barry only hired you because Borealis promised to support local business for the privilege of opening a diamond mine in the Northwest Territories. You are pushing your luck, big time." She jabbed the nail file at him for emphasis.

Gerald almost tossed his head again, but thought better of it. Hefting his briefcase onto the counter, he unloaded his jacket, a hunk of mountain-climbing rope and a snorkel. He squinted into the bag before removing his spectacles. "Super-strong reading glasses. All I could find in the bargain bin at the grocery store." He located an envelope and presented it to Krystal. "Security arrangements for the Diamond Gala – charity event of the year."

"What do you know about that?" Barry, director of Borealis's Northwest Territories operations, appeared behind Krystal and snatched the envelope from her hand. Barry's thin hair was sticking out at odd angles as if he had, indeed, been pulling at it. "Speak up, Gerald. How'd you know what's in here?"

"Elementary."

Barry's face turned a nasty shade of purple. He moved around the desk. "Have you been reading this? Is that what took so long?" Barry shook the envelope in the courier's face.

"Of course not."

"Nothing's a secret to an international man of mystery … and freelance waiter," Krystal said.

"Sit down while I call the RCMP."

Gerald's shoulders drooped. "I guessed. That's all. Everyone knows the Diamond Gala's coming up. The guys from your security company were at the hotel banquet rooms a couple of days ago deciding where to put the surveillance cameras. They were so paranoid this morning, I assumed the plans were in the envelope."

"You were snooping around the hotel?" The veins in Barry's temples were popping out.

"That's where I currently 'freelance,' as a waiter, as Krystal puts it."

"Waiter? You're such a lousy courier you have to moonlight as a waiter? To hell with my northern hiring quotas – you're fired."

"But I've kept your documents safe for months!"

"Your job is to walk them from Point A to Point B in the quickest time possible. That's it. Borealis's security is handled by actual trained professionals, who don't monkey around with this." Barry flipped Gerald's wig onto the ground. "Now get out!" Barry stormed into the sea of offices behind the reception desk.

Krystal snapped her gum. "Bummer," she said.

Gerald slumped into a chair. Krystal leaned over the reception desk to examine him.

"Get your suit at a flea sale?"

Gerald smoothed a sleeve. "Ya. Eight bucks at St. Pat's." He glanced up, his eyes catching on Krystal's cleavage. He fumbled around his left wrist. Krystal glanced at her exposed chest and jerked herself upright.

"Hand it over," she said.

"Hmm?"

"Now!"

Gerald unclasped what appeared to be a wristwatch and passed it to Krystal.

"I never should have told you I had a wrist camera," he said.

She pushed buttons until she found the digital photo of her cleavage, then erased it.

"Men. You're all the same." She tossed the camera back to him. "How can you afford this stuff, anyway? I'll call Radio Shack and say you're shoplifting. That'll fix you."

"Hey, I pay my way." Gerald pouted. "And no one complains when James Bond gets friendly with the babes."

"Here's some news: you're not James Bond. Now get out."

"I just wanted something to remember you by. This was the best job I ever had." A tear fell onto his suit as Gerald re-attached his wrist camera.

"Oh man, don't cry." Krystal looked away.

"I'm not." Gerald sniffled as he stuffed his jacket and spy accoutrement into his briefcase, then shuffled towards the door. He stopped beside a high-security display case and peered inside. There floated the show-piece of the Borealis jewellery collection, a necklace called the "North Wind," featuring the splashiest gems from the company's new mine up on the Northwest Territories barren-lands. The bottom of the L-shaped necklace was white gold, encrusted with tiny diamonds undulating like snowdrifts across a frozen lake. The diamonds arched into a stand of trees made of yellow gold, forming the arm of the L. From the treetops rose a shaman's face, cheeks puffed and mouth forming an "O" as he blew across the snow. Six large stones flew from his mouth like shooting stars.

"Worth half a million," Gerald said, wiping his nose on his sleeve.

Krystal fidgeted behind the counter. She came forward. "I'll tell you a secret about the gala – I'm going to be the Diamond Girl!"

"Cool."

"Barry's freaked about taking the necklace out in the open. A public relations firm convinced the board of directors to use the North Wind as the drawing card for the Diamond Gala. Just think – I'll be the first person to wear it." Krystal's nose hovered near the glass.

"You going to have a bodyguard?" Gerald asked.

"No. The organizers don't want to cramp the style of the Yellowknife ruling class. But you saw the cameras they're putting in. And there'll be security at the door. Besides, all the diamonds in the North Wind are laser-tattooed with a little moose. The necklace would be impossible to sell on the open market, either in one piece or broken up."

"There are such things as private collections."

Krystal straightened and scanned the lobby. "Don't be melodramatic."

On her way back to her desk, Krystal picked up Gerald's wig, lying forgotten on the floor. She twirled it in her fingers.

"Wanna have a drink tonight?"

"Who, me?" Gerald glanced around the empty lobby. "I thought you had a boyfriend."

"You mean Frank? Long gone."

Gerald sniffled. "And you want to have a drink with me?"

"IS THAT TWERP STILL HANGING AROUND?" Barry reappeared. His colour hadn't improved.

"He just won't leave," Krystal said loudly.

"Stop drooling on the display case and get away from the North Wind," Barry said.

Krystal marched over to Gerald. "Black Knight. Eight o'clock," she whispered, slipping the wig into his pocket so gently he barely felt it. She thumped him on the chest. "For the last time – get out!"

Gerald looked back as he scooted through the door. Krystal and Barry were watching him, arms crossed, and frowning.

• • •

GERALD WANDERED THE streets, spontaneously trailing people to keep up his skills. Not that it mattered anymore. Borealis Diamonds had been the first – and only – client of his courier business, his unique approach designed for the security needs of Canada's new diamond industry. He'd hoped his contract with Borealis would catapult him into a new life: safeguarding secret documents, changing disguises on the fly, canoodling with beautiful women. But now Barry had doomed him to the old routine: serving rubber chicken at banquets, hanging around Radio Shack, enduring the contempt of the women at the flower shop.

He touched the knife in his pocket. He'd let down his father, wherever he was, whatever he was doing. Gerald's mom had explained that his dad disappeared because of his job with the government, and instructed Gerald never to discuss the matter, with her or with anyone else. The seriousness of his father's mission was underscored when Gerald's mom burned all her husband's possessions, changed their last name, and moved to Yellowknife.

Gerald went home, put on a James Bond movie, and cried himself to sleep.

• • •

SHORTLY AFTER EIGHT o'clock, Gerald stepped into the Black Knight. Unable to locate Krystal in the crowded, murky pub, his fingers itched towards the night scope in his jacket pocket. A summer's worth of midnight sun had robbed him of the opportunity to use it.

The throng shifted as Gerald put the scope to his eye, revealing Krystal in a corner. He almost dropped it – a monstrous necklace gleaming above her neckline boosted her usual dazzle. A half-moon of yellow metal, sprinkled with rhinestones, was suspended from a thick chain. Up one side rose a pastiche created from old jewellery

– a clump of pine trees and some stars, topped by a gold Santa Claus face.

"Looks like the North Wind on acid," Gerald said.

"I made it myself. Found the bottom part at the drugstore, and the other bits and pieces in my drawer."

"It's quite … something."

Krystal smiled. "Thanks."

They ordered, and Gerald became aware of a set of eyes locked onto the back of his head. A thin, middle-aged man with a hawk-like nose was sitting at the next table, staring at him. Gerald flicked his scraggy hair out of his eyes and stared back. The guy likewise flicked his hair, and cracked his knuckles. Gerald dropped his gaze.

Their drinks appeared. One sip of his martini, and Gerald choked. "They bruised the gin," he spluttered. "Did you hear me say 'stirred, not shaken'?"

Krystal rolled her eyes. "Listen, Gerald. I've decided I need extra security when I'm the Diamond Girl. You working as a waiter at the gala?"

"Of course. They've had to hire extra staff."

"Good. I want you to double as my bodyguard."

"Really?" Gerald squirmed in his seat.

"As soon as I enter the banquet room, I want you to stick like glue. I can't pay you, but if you do this right, your future as a courier will be sealed."

"Always ready to help a damsel in distress." Gerald reached over and touched Krystal's hand. She withdrew it.

"What's your disguise?" she asked.

"Have to think about it."

"I need to know ahead of time. And Barry can't find out. He's particular about who I associate with."

"Why do you put up with him?"

Rifling through her shoulder bag, Krystal found a pack of cigarettes, lit up and exhaled a long, slow stream of smoke. "I needed a job, he liked my look, so he said he'd give me a chance."

"Liked your look? Barry notices things like that?"

"Oh, he has an eye for the ladies, alright. And the hands to go with."

Gerald shivered. "Gross."

Krystal shrugged. "Small price to pay. I'm just a receptionist now, but I want to be a designer." She touched her necklace. "An Armenian guy who's up here teaching diamond cutting said I'd be a natural, so that's my next step."

"Would Barry let you go? You'd need his recommendation."

"We play the Diamond Gala right, Barry will do whatever I want. Give me a pen, and I'll draw the banquet room." Krystal smoothed a napkin. Groping in his shirt, Gerald pulled out the first thing that came to hand – his new pen that could record a couple of short messages. Krystal was describing her grand entrance when someone appeared beside them. There stood Claire, hand on hip and eyebrows raised.

"Can I see you?" she said, steering Krystal towards a distant table. Claire did most of the talking, waving her hands and frowning towards Gerald. Krystal stared at the floor, nervously clicking the buttons on Gerald's pen. On her way back, the skinny man intercepted her. They spoke, and Krystal returned to Gerald, throwing the pen on the table so hard it bounced. Gerald shrieked.

"Gotta go." She reached for her cigarettes, knocking them to the floor. She scooped them into her purse, bumping Gerald's chair as she stood up.

"Take it easy, babe."

"Call me when you know what you're wearing." Krystal headed for the door, the skinny man on her heels. Gerald rose to follow, but Claire clamped onto his arm.

"Don't. Barry finds out you've been speaking, she'll be toast in the diamond biz."

"He has no right."

"Doesn't matter. That's why she and Frank broke up. Barry found out about Frank's record. Made him nervous."

"Frank cut a record?"

Claire stared at Gerald.

"Oh! You mean he's a criminal?" Gerald leaned closer. "A real one?"

"They do exist."

Gerald licked his lips. "What was he in for?"

"Embezzlement, if you must know. Skipped the country with his secretary. Got caught anyway." Claire released Gerald's arm. "Stay away from Krystal." She swished out of the pub.

Gerald sat down and inspected his pen. He clicked a button, and Claire's voice was back.

"… hell are you doing? He'll ruin you," she said

"… my chance to get rid of him … I'm sick of that loser," Krystal said before the recording chip cut out.

Wow, Gerald thought. *I didn't think she hated Barry that much.*

The other button was stuck. Gerald finished his martini, trudged home, and put the pen in his dresser drawer.

• • •

THE HOPE OF regaining the Borealis contract buoyed Gerald through the next few days as he searched for his night scope, which had gone missing, and as he visited and revisited Yellowknife's department stores and thrift shops to develop his new disguise. Two days before the Diamond Gala, he spent an hour in the bathroom, strapped on some padding, squeezed into his costume and examined himself in the mirror.

Perfect.

Gerald reached the mall by ten o'clock. Despite his inexperience with high heels, he looked half-way to sultry as he passed the flower store – neither Claire nor her co-worker batted an eye at the thin woman in the purple dress, black hair cut Cleopatra-style.

He found Krystal chatting with a friend in the coffee shop she frequented. Choosing a nearby table, Gerald stared over the top of his black-rimmed, purple-tinted glasses until Krystal glanced his way. She turned, then snapped back. Gerald winked.

Krystal drummed her fingers as her friend sipped her coffee. When the woman left, Krystal scanned the restaurant before joining Gerald. "What are you doing?"

"You wanted to know about the disguise."

"There are more discrete ways. A phone call. A Polaroid in a sealed envelope. You're the frigging spy – you figure it out."

Gerald grinned.

"Okay – stand up, but make it snappy." Gerald was in mid-twirl when a half snort, half scream erupted a couple of tables away. There sat the man from the bar, mopping up coffee he'd sprayed onto the table.

"What's his problem?" Gerald asked.

"Your skirt flipped up. I think he noticed your underwear."

"What's wrong with jockeys? I thought boxers would show with this hemline."

"They just bulge oddly for a female person. Are you going to serve drinks in that outfit?"

"Nope – black skirt, white shirt. Frumpy, but it's what all the waitresses are wearing this year." He smiled down at Krystal and batted his false eyelashes. "I couldn't resist the dress, though. Two dollars at the Sally Ann." Gerald became sombre. "Do I look like a floozie?"

Krystal reconsidered his outfit. "You're okay with pumps. Strappy shoes will make you look cheap."

"Mom's always ranting about floozies. Probably because of dad. But he has to cavort with beautiful women. It's part of his job."

"What does your dad do?"

Gerald reddened. "Never mind."

Krystal grabbed Gerald's arm and hoisted herself to her feet. "Give me a head start, then scram before anyone recognizes you." Krystal hurried away, the man from the bar stomping after her. Gerald would have followed, but his wrist camera was missing and he had to retrace his steps.

● ● ●

THE HOTEL CATERING manager rolled her eyes at Gerald's disguise as she handed him a tray of cutlery and sent him off to set tables for the gala. Northern lights shimmered in pink and green foil on the banquet room walls; fairy lights sparkled from the ceiling. The room's layout was as Krystal had described. Across the front stretched a platform. From its centre, a catwalk extended into a wooden dance floor, which was rimmed by the round tables Gerald was now setting.

Gerald soon found himself carrying tray after tray of champagne through the growing number of tuxedos and evening gowns. Krystal would be in the hotel's executive suite with the Borealis bigwigs, waiting to make her grand entrance. Barry was probably with them. Gerald was relieved he wouldn't have to see him until later in the evening.

"One of those for me?" a familiar voice whispered. Turning, he came face to face with Barry.

Gerald pushed his tinted glasses well up on his arched nose and held out the tray. As Barry helped himself, he slid a hand around

Gerald's waist. Gerald bit his lip. Barry ran the champagne glass under Gerald's chin and winked. He had just vacated Gerald's personal space when a robust woman in a black gown appeared.

"Thanks, dear," she said, lifting the champagne from Barry's hand. She frowned at Gerald, then grabbed her husband's elbow. "Time to shmooze," she said, leading him away.

Gerald almost collided with another waitress with Cleopatra hair as he escaped into the kitchen. He downed a couple of glasses of champagne, the horror of Barry's advances playing over and over in his mind.

"Hey – no slacking." The catering manager stood before him. "Didn't I just see you heading to the executive suite, Geraldine?"

"Hmm?" Gerald couldn't pause his mental video tape.

"Never mind. Fill your tray and get back out there."

The ceremonial drumming of the local First Nation greeted Gerald as he returned to the banquet room. His load of champagne vanished during several speeches, a fashion show, and songs of northern derring-do performed by men sporting plaid shirts and rubber boots. Unencumbered, he lurked by the stage until the master of ceremonies said: "And now, the moment you've all been waiting for – the Borealis Diamond Girl, and the North Wind."

The room went dark. A spotlight picked up Krystal at the end of the dais, wearing a silver lamé gown, pink lipstick, and a nervous smile. A golden shawl hid her neckline. With the exaggerated stroll of a model, she made her way to centre stage. Pausing, she tried to smile more broadly. As she flung open her shawl, the spotlight went out. Krystal screamed. Gerald was knocked to the floor.

When the lights came on, Krystal lay sprawled beside him. She sat up, and Gerald noticed her throat was bare. Then he noticed his night scope lay smashed between them.

Barry pushed through the crowd. He stared at Gerald, whose glasses and wig were askew.

"You ... you ... you!" He took a lungful of air. "GUARD!"

Gerald was frog-marched to the executive suite where Barry searched him.

"What's this?" Barry asked, pulling the North Wind from Gerald's pocket. Knees shaking, Gerald sunk onto the nearest couch. Guards stood nearby as Barry reviewed the security videos in the next room. Gerald squirmed.

"Feeling guilty?" one of the guards asked.

"No – this bra is killing me."

The man stared at Gerald's chest. Gerald crossed his arms protectively.

"Men," he said. "You're all the same."

"Gotcha!" Barry marched into the room, the North Wind dangling from his fingers. "We have you on tape, bringing a tray of drinks to the executive suite. That must be when you stole it."

"But I never came here."

"No mistaking the wig or that schnozz of yours. I'm getting rid of you once and for all, you loser."

Gerald gasped. "Krystal set me up! She wanted to seal my fate as a courier!" He pulled out his recording pen, clicked a button, and Krystal's voice said, "... my chance to get rid of him ... I'm sick of that loser."

Krystal's dress rustled as she entered, flanked by security guards. She was pale, and her make-up did not mask the dark circles under her eyes. "You're not the loser I was talking about, Gerald. Keep blithering, though, and I'll change my mind. I was talking about Frank. He was sitting behind you that night in the bar." She moved forward. "Thank heaven the necklace is safe."

Barry clutched the North Wind and retreated a step. "You said you'd dropped Frank."

There was a ruckus at the door. A security guard re-appeared and pushed the other Cleopatra-coiffed waitress onto the couch beside Gerald.

"Hey, there sister-friend," Gerald said.

The waitress's lip curled in scorn. She took off her purple-tinted glasses and scrutinized Gerald.

"Didn't I say he looked like you, Frank?" Krystal said.

"About twenty-five years ago," the 'waitress' said in a baritone, pulling off his wig.

"Found him lurking around the back door – with this." A security guard flashed the copy of the North Wind that Krystal had worn in the bar.

"It's not illegal to have a necklace like that," Frank said.

Barry inspected it. "Should be."

"Came back for the real one, didn't you?" Krystal asked.

Frank flicked his eyes towards the North Wind, still clutched in Barry's hand. Then he shifted his weight and pulled a small object from beneath him. It was a multi-blade knife.

"I used to have a model just like this," Frank said.

"Hey! That's my James Bond knife." Gerald grabbed at it, but a security guard intercepted.

Frank's complexion took on a greyish tinge. "What'd you call it?"

"Actually, it's my dad's James Bond knife."

"Oh, good God. You're *that* Gerald. How did you end up in Yellowknife?"

Gerald peered at him. "Dad?"

Frank's pallor progressed into a shade of green. Gerald bounced closer on the couch.

"Dad! Look – I'm just like you. I'm James Bond."

Frank recoiled. "James Bond is a lady's man. Not a girlie-man. He never dressed like a broad."

Gerald's eyes went round. His top lip quivered.

"You're such a jerk, Frank." Krystal turned to Barry. "He's the one who came up to the suite."

"Prove it," Frank said.

Krystal pulled Gerald's wrist camera from her purse. Gerald's eyebrows contracted for a few moments. "You took that at the coffee shop!"

"And I took your night scope in the bar," she said, pressing buttons on the tiny camera.

"Haven't lost your touch, I see," Frank said.

"What?" Barry said.

Krystal glared at Frank. He sneered back. Krystal took a deep breath. "I used to pick pockets, Barry. I was very good, but I eventually got caught."

"But your security check – "

Krystal shook her head. "I was a young offender. My records are sealed."

"You're fired."

"Just listen. Frank knew me in those days. He knew you wouldn't be thrilled to have a former thief working for you. When he heard I was going to be the Diamond Girl, he insisted I help him steal the North Wind, or he'd tell you about my shady past. And that would be it for me in the diamond business."

Frank shook his head. "Some story. You're just ticked I dumped you."

Krystal gave the camera to Barry. "See. He's here in the executive suite. When Frank delivered the drinks, I ducked into the bathroom, wrapped the North Wind in toilet paper and tucked it into his pocket. I kept my neck covered until I went downstairs. When the lights went out, I was supposed to plant the fake on Gerald – that's why I needed the night scope. Frank would make his getaway while everyone tried figure out where the real necklace was, and how Yellowknife's favourite spy was involved. But I swapped them to keep the North Wind safe."

Frank snorted. "You are one bitter and twisted woman."

"You have to believe me, Barry. I couldn't shake Frank, and he would have tried to steal it with or without me. He had a private collector. I had to stage a fake theft to prove I'm trustworthy."

"You and Gerald were caught red-handed." Barry's eyes wandered over Krystal's silver-clad figure. "I'll miss having you around."

Krystal's head drooped. "I'm sorry, Gerald."

Shoulders hunched, Gerald was fiddling with his spy pen. "You broke it that night," he grumbled. There was a snap, then came Frank's recorded voice.

" … better not double-cross me, you stupid cow. I don't get the North Wind, you don't get a future. Got it?"

"Dad!" Gerald said. "That's not nice."

"Stop calling me that, you freak."

Gerald's face crumpled, then abruptly smoothed itself out. His eyes narrowed. "I thought you worked for the government."

"Until I stole a couple million dollars."

"And took off with some floozie."

"Ya?"

"Leaving me and mom on our own."

"So?"

Krystal's purse sat on the coffee table. Gerald grabbed it and got in three or four blows before the security guards hauled his father to safety. Barry, Krystal and Gerald remained in the room.

"You're still fired," Barry told Krystal.

"I don't think so. What about your wandering hands? Your wife would want to know about that."

"You go, girl," Gerald said.

"My word against yours," Barry said.

"She'll believe us," Gerald said. "She already suspects."

"Us?" Krystal asked.

A security guard returned. "Barry – everyone's waiting for the North Wind. And the RCMP phoned to see if everything's alright. They're getting calls." The guard glanced at Gerald and Krystal, then leaned close to Barry. "And your wife wants to know what you're doing up here with a couple of floozies."

Gerald squeaked in protest. Sweat glistened on Barry's forehead.

"We'll talk terms later," Krystal said as Barry relinquished the necklace. "One thing's for sure – the Diamond Girl needs a body-guard." Krystal cast an eye over Gerald's uniform. "You want to put on something else, seeing as how James Bond never dressed like a woman?"

"To hell with James Bond. But I do want to get out of these drab duds." Gerald's eyes glittered. "I brought the purple dress. It's downstairs."

Krystal grinned. "You go girl," she said, as Gerald ran to change.

Marty Gervais

The Lexicon of Snoring

We lie side by side
in hospital beds
opposite one another
He tells me my snoring
is like a battered room
air conditioner kicking in
from time to time
I tell him his snoring
is like a fishing boat
yawing in a stormy harbour
We blow and grind
in our own ways
like lazy whales uneasy
and aimless in the north sea
We sputter like Spitfires
in our sleep, the rising
and falling of guttural
noises, diving low and
soaring high, bombing
villages and factories
and dogfighting enemy
planes, and bearing
the babel of sleep from deep
within us, nightmares
dreams, hopes, regrets
the overtures roll like
tumbleweed across
an open prairie
and we're running
into the wind as the
sky swirls into a storm
all black and gray
like a bruise on
the arm, and we
feel the headlong
day and the tide

of the moment
We snore like politicians
on the hustings
making sense of nothing
blather and jabber
in the chaos, and go right on
caring nothing if anyone
hears our message
We snore and we snore
and we snore like evangelists
flipping frantically for
the right chapter and verse
then sputtering it out
in pressing and insistent refrains
We snore and we snore
and we snore in
prolonged stretches
like a breakaway
to the net, our bodies
poised and never yielding
till that precise moment
when we let the puck fly
into the twine
We snore and we
snore and we gasp
and we puff and
we heave, lifting ourselves
higher and higher then
sinking and falling and
rising again, slowly
advancing like a huffing
steam engine picking up
speed and suddenly roaring
for all its worth and then
we're backtracking
in muffled grunts
like disgruntled old boars in the yard
and we snore and we snore
and we snore...

Marty Gervais

This is what I know about penises

For J.B.L.

I have always had a little
trouble making it plural,
The word doesn't look right
when you add "es"
Doesn't sound right
to have more than one
at any one time
though there was a doctor
in 1609 in Wecker
who found a corpse
in Bologna with two penises
I lie in the bathtub
and think about what
you told me today
how you decided
to write an ode to your penis
as if it was your best friend
and wonder if Keats or
Shelly might've pondered
the same. Or how you
carry it with you
like a badge from
a secret society
how it never lets you down
But have you forgotten
those childhood years
when you wet the bed
at a sleepover at a friend's
Or those times
in the schoolyard
when you weren't looking,
and someone tossed a football

and you bent over double
as the pain shot through you
like an electric charge
Or those moments
after so much adolescent
fumbling in the back seat
of a car, you lay back
sweating and humiliated
because at long last
you couldn't get it up
you couldn't make it work
Or those porno films
that made you believe
you were the only one
in the world that small —
I lie in the bathtub
and stare at my own —
it bobs in the soapy water
like an arrogant swimmer
and think of all the
names given it
over the centuries —
knob, dick, shumck, rod
tool, percy, John Thomas,
the bald headed mouse, the
yoghurt-spitting sausage,
Kojack's Moneybox,
the salty salami, Sergeant
with one blue stripe
who loves to stand
at attention, Captain Winky
the pink lighthouse that wants
to draw you onto its rocks
the sentimental teaser, the arrow
of desire, the crimson butterfly
the flute of love and
the blood-gorged meat club
I lie in the bathtub and

stare as it, as if it was
a neighbour's dog
that wouldn't stop barking
as if it was a car that suddenly
spun out of control
and struck a telephone pole
as if it was a new face at
school, someone else
to ridicule and mock
I think of penis sizes
the average being 3.5 inches
the longest 13 inches
how a man will average
11 erections in a day
and 9 at night, and
how in a life time
he will ejaculate 7,200 times
I think of the ancient Greeks
who worshipped it,
and paraded the streets
of Athens with six-foot phalluses
how the early Christians
saw it as the Devil's Rod
a thing of evil shape
how every March 15
the Japanese in the
small town of Komaki
throw a giant
festival to celebrate the penis
and parade the streets
with a 900-pound
phallus, and how women
carry massive dildos
in their arms
how the Caramjoa tribe
of Northern Uganda
tie a weight on the end
of their penises

to elongate it
how the men of the Walibri
tribe of central Australia
greet each other
by shaking penises
instead of hands
I think of the questions
surrounding it —
Is size important?
If not, why are
there no two-inch
pencil-thin vibrators?
Why would men rather lose
a leg than the family
jewels? Is masturbation
exciting because it is sex
with someone you pity?
And just who is the
captain of the ship?
Tell me ...
I lie in the bathtub
and wonder if it
could ever really be someone
else's best new friend ...

B.D. Miller

Ivory Majesto's Eye-Poppin', Stomach-Turnin', Faith-Shatterin' Freak Show

THE FREAKS GOT into town under a feeble moon, parked their bus lengthwise on Main, and checked into the top three floors of the Slocumb Hotel. It was the first time the hotel had been full up since the Barley Growers' Convention of '22, and Innkeeper Willie could hardly believe his luck when he came downstairs at five minutes to six and checked the register. Nobody had seen them come except Ninety-Proof Charlie, the desk clerk who worked midnight to seven-thirty.

Willie decided to keep his mouth shut about the freaks, but all hell broke loose at ten past seven when one of the breakfast regulars at Rumpel's Café spotted the bus—all purple and orange and canary yellow, with big red letters on the sides promising the scariest freaks this side of the Mississippi. The townsfolk poured out of the café and crowded into the hotel lobby, demanding to know all the hideous details.

"Is they scary?"

"Is they deformed?"

"Is there midgets and monkey boys and bearded ladies?"

Willie deferred all questions to Ninety-Proof Charlie.

"They seemed like honest folk," old Charlie said, wishing everyone would just go away and leave him alone, or at least stop talking so loudly.

Charlie was half blind from glaucoma and cataracts, and hardly ever sober, and not much interested in freaks or anything else ever since his wife had died of a burst appendix three summers previous. Truth was, old Charlie couldn't remember much of anything about the night before, having spent most of his shift pouring four-star whiskey into a dirty cup. He did remember a rather handsome man with a goatee and a handlebar mustache and an English or maybe Australian accent.

"A real nice fella," Charlie said. "He was wearing some sort of cape. Red with gold lining, if I remember right."

But the townsfolk didn't care to hear about some cape-clad visitor from England or maybe Australia. "Tell us more about the freaks," they kept imploring and poor old Charlie just kept on shrugging.

Willie and a posse of townsfolk climbed the hotel stairs and walked up and down the halls of the top three floors, but all the doors were deadbolted and had DO NOT DISTURB signs on the brass knobs. "We'd better let them be," whispered Willie, hotel keys jangling on a big metal ring. "They probably need their beauty sleep." And the posse headed back downstairs, pouring out onto Main to inspect the freak show bus.

"What kinda low-grade freaks would come to this town anyways?" asked Sneering Jimmy Dudley, walking around and around the bus, kicking the tires and scratching his armpit with a coffee spoon. Sneering Jimmy was the town skeptic. "You want to see some freaks, go to Saskatoon and walk around the downtown on a Saturday night. Then you'll see some freaks," said Sneering Jimmy.

"Oh, I dunno, this town has had some pretty big attractions over the years," countered Booster Bill McFadden, the mayor of Slocumb, who was standing on tip-toes in front of the bus, fingers wrapped around the radiator grille and nose pressed to the windshield glass. "Remember the town fair in ought seven? We had people coming from as far away as Swift Current."

"Hey Scoop!" someone shouted. "What'cha figure?"

Everybody turned to look at a tiny pink man in a smelly tweed jacket who was standing by the back of the bus, scribbling furiously in a dog-eared notepad. Scoop Crabtree was editor of the Slocumb Scavenger and he knew hard news when it slapped him in the face. He'd broken the story about Lucinda Pomeroy's record-setting pumpkin way back in 1915, and some of his articles had even been picked up by the big city papers.

"Freaks take over Slocumb," Scoop muttered darkly to no one in particular, and kept on scribbling. "We just may have to print a special edition." The last time the Slocumb *Scavenger* had printed a special edition was the Armistice in 1918. Scoop kicked the mud off the rear bumper of the bus and inspected the license plate. "Hey, they're from Missouri!" he shouted, and the townsfolk all crowded around, whispering loudly.

"Nothing but Grade A freaks come outta Missouri," said Hagglin' Hesper, the butcher's wife, who'd never been south of the forty-ninth parallel her whole life.

"I think I just saw one of the freaks in the window!" somebody shouted from across the street, and the townsfolk all rushed into the middle of Main for a better look, nearly forcing a milk truck from McCrackin's Cheese and Dairy to run over a lamp post. "The far left window on the top floor," said Pickler Pete Merriman, the local mortician, jabbing a finger in the air. "Honest to God, I seen somebody looking down from behind the blinds."

"That's the Presidential Suite," Willie said proudly. "I'll bet that's where the King of the Freaks is staying."

The townsfolk stood in the middle of Main, necks bent and jaws on the ground for a good half hour, staring at the pulled blinds on the top three floors of the hotel. They would have stared longer, but a few minutes past eight o'clock a rather handsome man with a goatee and a handlebar mustache came jouncing down the hotel steps and onto the sidewalk, jabbing at the cracks in the concrete with a silver-tipped walking cane, red and gold cape trailing behind his shoulders. The stranger tipped his bowler at the townsfolk and strode down Main, past Pickler Pete's funeral parlour and Geiger's Shop-n-Go Grocery, angling across the street toward Rumpel's Café.

"Hey, maybe *he* saw the freaks!" shouted Hagglin' Hesper, and the townsfolk all rushed to the café, watching through the window as the caped stranger sat down on a stool and ordered bacon and eggs with wheat toast, hashbrowns extra crispy, and a side-order of buttermilk pancakes. They kept on staring as the stranger positioned his bowler just so on the counter, flipped open a yellowed copy of the *St. Louis Post-Dispatch* and buried his nose in the baseball summaries, waiting for the eggs to fry.

"Maybe somebody should go in and ask," suggested Pickler Pete.

"It's not polite to bother somebody while they're eating," said Hagglin' Hesper.

"He ain't eating just yet," said Booster Bill, who hadn't won seven mayoralty elections in a row for being an idiot. The townsfolk nodded approvingly and as many of them as could fit followed Booster Bill into the café.

"Pardon me, sir, but do you know anything about the freaks?" asked the mayor, a little embarrassed by his own question.

The stranger smiled, put down his newspaper, and rose from the stool. "I certainly do my good man," the stranger said, in a thick English or maybe Australian accent. "Allow me to introduce myself." He straightened his cape and bowed deeply. "The name's Majesto. Ivory Majesto. Renaissance man, raconteur and sole proprietor of Ivory Majesto's Eye-Poppin', Stomach-Turnin', Faith-Shatterin' Freak Show."

The townsfolk in the café all started clapping and cheering and asking a million questions at once. "When do we get to see the freaks?" asked Pickler Pete.

"All in good time, my good man, all in good time," said Ivory Majesto, busting at the seams from all the attention.

"What kinda freaks you got?" asked Sneering Jimmy, hands on hips.

"Oh, all kinds, sir. The finest freaks of every description," Ivory said. "Freaks so hideous and grotesque, they'll shake your faith in God."

Scoop Crabtree cleared his throat and the café suddenly fell silent. You couldn't put nothing past old Scoop and the townsfolk loved watching him in action. "My good man," Scoop said, pencil poised at the top of his notepad and doing his best to mock the stranger's accent. "What's an Englishman doing in these parts, driving a bus from Missouri?"

"Oh *that*," said Ivory Majesto, shifting his eyes about the café and rolling the ends of his mustache with twitchy fingers. "Well, now. I inherited the show from an American uncle in Saint Louie and came across the pond in '23 to keep up the family tradition. I've lived on this side of the Atlantic ever since, but can't seem to lose this dratted accent. The ladies find it charming, fortunately." Ivory winked at Hagglin' Hesper and she winked back and started to giggle.

"You got any bearded ladies? You got any midgets?" asked little Joey Geiger, the grocer's son.

"Do we have midgets? My boy, we've got midgets *this* big," Ivory said, flipping his cape in the air and levitating the palm of one hand about a foot off the floor. "I'll throw up a few flyers this afternoon," he promised. "Let you good people in on all the details. But until then, may I enjoy some of your down-home hospitality?" Ivory waved a hand at the counter where the waitress had just set down his eggs.

"Oh, certainly, by all means," said Booster Bill. "I'm sure you'll find the hospitality in Slocumb second to none." And the townsfolk all poured back into the street, whispering loudly.

But the flyers didn't go up that afternoon, or the following day, or the day after that either. The shades stayed down and the doors stayed locked on the top three floors of the Slocumb Hotel, and Willie was too scared of the freaks to use his pass key. Ivory Majesto spent most of his time walking back and forth between the café and the hotel beer parlour, putting everything on a tab and charming the ladies of the town with compliments and entertaining the men with ribald tales of his trips to Siberia and the upper Amazon and deepest, darkest Africa to look for freaks.

On the third day, Booster Bill asked Ivory, between pitchers of beer, when the townsfolk might expect to see the show. Ivory drained his glass and snapped his fingers at the waitress, before smoothing his goatee with the palm of one hand. "My good man, the thing you have to remember about freaks," he said, "is you can't push them. They're freaks after all and they've got a lot on their minds. We've had a long drive up from Missouri and my freaks are dreadfully tired. They can barely pry their heads off the pillows."

Booster Bill nodded sympathetically.

"But I think another day's bedrest should do the trick," Ivory said, pinching the waitress high up on the thigh as she set down a fresh pitcher of beer.

Two more days went by and Ivory Majesto kept running up tabs all over town. Nasty rumours started cropping up on coffee row that certain ladies of the town had begun visiting Ivory late at night in the Presidential Suite of the Slocumb Hotel. One rumour even had Bottoms-Up Betty, the wife of Booster Bill, paying Ivory a visit. Just as the men of the town had decided enough was enough and were going to rush the top floor of the hotel with pitchforks, Ivory Majesto ambled over to Rumpel's Café and started taping a poster inside the front window. The poster was the same colour as the freak show bus—all purple and orange and canary yellow, with big red letters.

"COMING SOON!" the poster screamed. "The scariest freaks this side of the Mississippi!" Underneath, in smaller type, were gruesome descriptions of the freaks—everything from a bearded, eight-hundred-pound lady to a two-headed man with the legs and body of a goat to a midget who slept in a matchbox. Ivory finished taping the poster to the window and sat at the counter, ordering a sirloin steak with fried onions, a side-order of baby potatoes, and two slices of lemon meringue pie for dessert. While he ate, the townsfolk crowded around the window, reading the poster with busy lips and nodding approvingly.

The next morning, rumours were thick all over town that Hayroll Holly, the preacher's daughter, had spent the night in the Presidential Suite doing God knows what with Ivory Majesto. Like a lot of girls raised on the Bible and the toe of her father's boot, Holly had developed a fanatical interpretation of "Love Thy Neighbour"—and Ivory was by no means the first man in town to receive her ministrations. But he was the first Preacher Bob ever found out about, and when the minister heard his daughter was up in the Presidential Suite he started pacing in front of the hotel, mad as a grizzly, craning his neck at the drawn blinds. Holly didn't come down until a quarter past ten in the morning, and by then there was a rut in the middle of Main fifteen yards long and three feet deep from Preacher Bob's pacing.

"What do you have to say for yourself, young lady?" Preacher Bob asked his daughter, wagging a long, thin finger under her nose.

"We just talked, that's all," Holly said, checking to make sure her sweater wasn't on inside out.

"Yes, yes, we'll talk about that later," said Preacher Bob. "Now tell me, did you see anything of the freaks?"

Holly stopped tugging at her sweater and wrinkled her forehead. "He wouldn't show me the freaks," she said vexedly, protruding her lower lip like a kid who'd had her lollipop taken away. "He said they're not rested yet. He said maybe next week."

The townsfolk who'd gathered around all groaned and rolled their eyes and a few of them started cursing right in front of Preacher Bob. "Goll darn it," swore Booster Bill. "Running up tabs and sleeping with our wives and daughters is one thing. But making us wait another week to see the freaks is inexcusable." And the townsfolk all started shouting and cursing and arguing, right in the middle of Main, until Booster Bill went and grabbed a pitchfork, leading the rush up the steps of the Slocumb Hotel. Willie headed off the mob with a cocked shotgun, saying there'd be no violence on his premises—at least not until he'd had a chance to talk things over with Ivory Majesto. As soon as the mob had calmed down, Willie turned heel and headed up the stairs to the top floor of the hotel.

"You gotta do something, Ivory," Willie said, sitting on the gigantic coil-spring bed of the Presidential Suite as Ivory Majesto trimmed his goatee in front of the bathroom mirror. "The townsfolk is out for blood. You'd better bring out the freaks, or they're gonna ride you outta town on a rail."

"All right, all right," Ivory said, working fresh wax into the ends of his handlebar mustache. "Tell them tonight they're going to see the scariest freaks this side of the Mississippi."

Ivory spent the rest of the morning walking all over town, flipping his cape in the air and looking for just the right venue for his freak show. He finally settled on the old curling rink next to the highway approach. Ivory had the men of the town drag in as much lumber and scrap metal as they could lay their hands on, ordering them to start building a stage in the center of the rink, with cages and partitions and trap doors. The women and children of Slocumb pitched in too—sewing curtains for the fronts of the cages, sweeping the cobwebs off the bleachers, and painting everything in sight all purple and orange and canary yellow. There hadn't been so much excitement at the Slocumb curling rink since the winter of '28, when the town had a Victory Reception for Hammertoss Findlater, who was fourth runner-up that year at the Tankard. The townsfolk didn't notice that they were doing all the work and that Ivory Majesto spent most of his time sitting in the bleachers with his feet up, drinking lemonade and chatting up all the pretty girls.

By late afternoon the renovations were complete, and the townsfolk could barely contain their excitement waiting for the show to begin. They started milling around and around the curling rink right after supper, two hours before showtime, speculating about the freaks and placing bets on which of the ladies of the town would be the first to faint or run home shrieking when the curtains went up. Meanwhile, Ivory Majesto was back at the café, pinching the waitresses high up on the thigh and enjoying a supper of roast pork with applesauce, a side order of buttered parsnips, and two heaping bowls of strawberries and cream for dessert.

Around seven-thirty, Ivory walked down to the curling rink, cape trailing behind his shoulders, jabbing the dirt with his walking cane. He was carrying a strongbox for the gate receipts, and he set up shop outside the rink's main entrance. "Step right up! Step right up!" Ivory shouted. "Only two dollars a head to see the scariest freaks this side of the Mississippi."

"Two dollars!" exclaimed Hagglin' Hesper. "That's a little steep, don't you think? A movie only costs a dime."

"If these were ordinary freaks, I'd agree with you entirely, my dear," Ivory said. "But these freaks will curl your hair three times over. Satisfaction guaranteed or your money refunded."

"Oh, *well*," said Hagglin' Hesper. "I didn't know there was a money-back guarantee." And the townsfolk started pouring into the curling rink at two dollars a crack, jamming the bleachers to the rafters—talking and laughing and tittering, all nervous and excited.

At precisely seven minutes past eight o'clock the lights dimmed and Ivory Majesto stepped on stage into a blue spotlight, clapping his hands for silence. "Ladies and gentlemen, children of all ages! Prepare to witness the *stupidest* freaks this side of the Mississippi!" he shouted, before vanishing down one of the trap doors.

Booster Bill leaned over to Bottoms-Up Betty and whispered, "I think he meant to say *scariest* freaks—," but his wife shushed him up.

And then the stage started creaking and the metal cages started rattling and the curtains started swaying until the entire fabrication collapsed in a heap on the floor of the curling rink. When the dust settled the people of Slocumb sat staring from the bleachers at one another for a good five minutes. They would have stared longer, but Pickler Pete thought he heard a bus rumble past on the highway approach. The townsfolk rushed out of the curling rink in time to see Ivory wheeling his purple and orange and canary yellow bus onto the highway. He gave a quick wave to the crowd and started bouncing down the Number One in the general direction of Fairweather and the setting sun.

"What'cha figure, Scoop?" somebody asked, and the townsfolk all crowded around, whispering loudly.

"I figure we been had," said Scoop Crabtree, squinting into the sun and scribbling furiously in his notepad. You couldn't put nothing past old Scoop.

"Maybe we should call the folks in Fairweather and warn them or something," suggested Willie.

"Naw, let them find out for themselves," said Booster Bill, kicking the dirt with his boots.

And then the townsfolk all turned to Sneering Jimmy Dudley, the town skeptic, looking like children who knew they were going to get spanked and wanting to get it over with.

"Well, what are you waiting for?" asked Hagglin' Hesper. "Aren't you gonna say, 'I told you so?'"

But Sneering Jimmy just shrugged. "All I know," he said finally, tugging at a stinkweed, "is these past few days has been more entertaining than downtown Saskatoon on a Saturday night." And the townsfolk all nodded approvingly and started the long walk back to the café.

Richard Stevenson

Canada Geese Nesting Site

" these geese are here for your viewing pleasure"
— Henderson Lake Parks sign

And now, ladies and gentlemen,
direct from Lake Tahoe,
here on the back swing
of their sell-out western tour –
for one spring only! —
the quintessentially Canadian,
the very excellent,
the sleek and radiant
father and mother act
you've been waiting
all winter to see –
the Canada Geese!

Honk! Honk! Yes, thank you, thank you.
Wonderful to be here
in your fair city of – what? —
Honk! Honk! Lethbridge is it? Yes.
Well, wonderful, just wonderful.
Honk! And nice to see
so many of you fine folks
bundled up, walking past
our little island community — honk! —
with dogs and kids in tow – honk! —
on roller blades and jogging.
Honk! Honk! We thought
we'd share that lovely spring ritual –
honk! — that very goosey business
of goosing the missus and – honk! —
procreating for you all – honk! —
and shell out a few goslings
for this – honk! honk! — gaggle of groupies

you might say. Honk! Honk! Harrggghhhh –
Ahhh – Sorry, a little indigestion.
Didn't mean to foul the nestin'.
Honk! Honk! Well, you know –
loose as a goose, as they say –
even the great Caruso
got to clear his throat
before he sang. Har! Har! Honk!
Honk! Honk! Honk! Honk!

shereen inayatulla

Love on Piss

Meredith and Paul Corban had been married for 8 years and 4 months when Meredith left the note on the bathroom mirror.

Hon,   *2:14am*
If you leave the toilet seat up just one more time, I will divorce you.
                  Sitting in a bowl of my own piss,
                  Me(redith)

She meant it too. O did she ever mean it.

Later that day, Paul phoned the shrink.
"It's a toilet seat. It's a goddamn toilet seat. That's it. That's all."
The shrink gave a sympathetic nod even though they were on the phone and Paul couldn't see it.
When Meredith came home from work that evening, Paul was wearing only an apron. They had sex on the kitchen floor.

The following week, Meredith had lunch with her co-worker.
"He never said anything about the note. But I think it may have done the trick. The seat has been faithfully down ever since."
"And how's the sex?" inquired the co-worker.
"Out of this world," Meredith said as she finished her dill pickle.

That night, Meredith found Paul's hand-written, cardboard sign hanging from the bathroom door.

Caution:
If you are a lady about to use this toilet, please be certain to return the seat to its elevated position for other people's personal convenience.
                  Thank you kindly,
                  The Man Of The House

Meredith phoned the shrink.
"A toilet seat. Patriarchy. Misogyny. Penis envy? (Hee hee hoo hoo) hah! Where's my chainsaw when I need it?"
The shrink said, "Hmmm."

That night, Meredith and Paul did it in the walk-in-closet.

Throughout the week, Meredith kept leaving the seat down and Paul kept leaving it up. They didn't exchange a word on the matter.

The following Saturday, Meredith put on her purple sweatpants (shopping gear) and hit the hardware store. Paul spent the afternoon in his hammock. When he came in around dinnertime, he found the toilet seat Crazy Glued down.

Paul: "Maniac. Lunatic. Out-right-witch."
Shrink: "It sounds like you're angry."

They had t-bone steak for dinner. They discussed the brewing tension in the Middle East. But neither Meredith nor Paul mentioned their toilet.

Later that night, Meredith crawled into bed in her leopard print nightgown. Paul was already naked. They both fell asleep during the 9:00 news. But when they woke up they had a quickie on the nightstand before work.

Summer came and went. Pine cones rolled around on the ground. The leaves aged in the autumn air and shriveled and curled and fell off the trees.

Meredith left town on business. It was just the opportunity Paul had been seeking.

When Meredith returned, there was no note. There was no sign. There was no toilet either. It had been replaced by a brand new, shiny, white urinal. Paul had had it installed that very morning.

Meredith took the meat tenderizer from the kitchen and smashed the urinal to pieces. For the next 24 hours they had to pee in the shower and avoid eating bran. But the sex was better than ever.

Then Paul called the repairperson.
"A meat tenderizer? Sir...I'm afraid that's going to cost you."

And cost him it did.

A year later, Meredith and the repairperson were married while Paul recovered from the surgery on his congested bowels.

(But as Meredith discovered on their honeymoon, the repairperson turned out to be impotent hee hee hoo hoo hah.)

The shrink closed The Corban File and flushed.

Shelley L. Kozlowski

Unhinged

TOO LATE, I discover the only renovation advice one should ever follow on a whim lies along the lines of, "A potted palm would look nice there," or, "Installing a brighter light bulb should do the trick."

Standing in the battle-scarred ruins of my once-charming 55-year-old kitchen, I am haunted by my brother's genial suggestion of six months ago: "Gee, did you know your hinges are chrome under all this paint? You really should show them off."

After tossing this idea around for some months, I finally realized how chic, how very retro, forty deco-styled, mini chrome fenders would look locked in formation on my very own kitchen cabinets. *Yes,* I thought, *I could win contests for this!* I could visualize the sun glinting off my hinges as my kitchen swarmed with photographers on assignment from interior design magazines snapping away for just the right shot to capture the very essence of my award-winning restoration.

Today, I can't imagine completion date. It's taken me three long days to dig out 200 screws from under no less than five layers of paint, the walls creaking and groaning as they begrudgingly set each screw free. As each hinge crisply snaps away from the wall, I'm left with yet another nation's coastal outline, in bas-relief. There are deep gouges in the walls from slipped screwdrivers, and I'm wondering if I should get a tetanus shot for the wound on my hand.

I wash my face, wrap a towel around my still-bleeding hand, and make my way to the friendly neighborhood hardware store. Too exhausted to explain my predicament, I can only bleat "Help!" and point weakly with my over-sized bandage at the hinge held in my good hand. Obviously well trained in the do-it-yourselfer's short-hand form of communication, an efficient staff member has me lined up at the cashier in mere moments with a new, environmentally friendly paint remover.

"Chrome," I waggle my eyebrows at the cashier, expecting a gush of envy.

"So I see," he waggles back, unimpressed.

My enthusiasm not yet crushed, I return to the combat zone and sand away at my maps of Peru and the Baja while my hinges soak in the remover. Then I'm gripped with a sudden wave of panic: Didn't they use lead in their paints way back when? Afraid to take chances, I rush back to the hardware store for a facemask, as well as make a stop at the pharmacy for proper bandages.

The next day, after my initial painful attempt at scraping the blistered paint from my hinges, I read the directions on the paint-remover bottle. Sure enough, 'chemical- resistant stripping gloves' are required. As well as protective lenses. Back to the hardware store.

Looking for someone to blame for the loss of my fingerprints, I approach yesterday's Mr. Efficiency.

"I didn't realize the paint remover you sold me yesterday required special equipment," I state, with undertones of accusation.

"Hm. Imagine that," he replies.

He glides away to leave me thinking, *Awfully blasé for someone surrounded by so many sharp instruments, including that ax.* However, rather than face a term in the Correctional Centre for Women, I make my purchases and return home to my important task awaiting me.

Once home, I realize how Neil Armstrong must have felt, preparing for that famous giant step - wearing the protective gear greatly reduces visibility and manipulation. But I plod through and scrape, clean, wash, and lovingly line up my hinges, ready to go, once I touch up the paint where I've had to sand away the coastal images.

Now that the light at the end of the tunnel is clearly within sight, I find myself actually singing as I rummage for the tin of paint marked 'kitchen'. I whip out my brush and delicately feather in the fresh paint. As I stand back to admire my handiwork, the truth becomes glaringly obvious: my kitchen paint has changed color. Since the last time I painted - three years ago - the insipid beige of the former owner's taste has seeped through my own glacial blue selection. It now looks to be vile turquoise in comparison to the fresh patches.

CURSES!

Back at the hardware store, I load up on brushes, rollers, trays, gloves, undercoat, and a fresh gallon of blue paint. The cashier very generously throws in a painter's cap - gratis. My lucky day.

In the end, my two-day project (three, tops!) has taken me two and a half weeks to complete, including clean up. I have forgiven my brother after another two weeks, and invite him over to view my accomplishment.

"Hey! Nice work," he says, and I'm proud of all the time I've put into restoring the kitchen to it's former glory.

"Gee," he says, "did you know you have hardwood under this carpet?"

John B. Lee

What Is Is

Monica
takes a long and breathless draw
on the brown cigar of everyone's America

darkens the paper tip
with an only slightly
moist glissando of her silken similitude
as one might
dip dry cedar
or watch
the slow absorption
of water rising on a river reed

this woman
opens like old tobacco
pupating
to the sea-spice of her own
redolent well
seducing that fragrant weed
with a deep and lovely allure...

as if she were only famous
for one desire, as if she were only
the walking humidor, only
the place we keep to keep our
best Havanas in, why then
who would not be satisfied, who then
among the hand-rolled men
mulling their unsmoked smokes
in women would not
elect as we elect
entire Californias
when the tide is high
and the moon-shocked window cleaners
catch their buckets full
on the silvery fin-wet winds
where the dolphins fly
thinking themselves to be
the long-lost bottle-nosed princes of France.

John B. Lee

One Walkie Talkie

Last evening
a man told me
he got a good deal
when he bought
at a barn sale
one walkie talkie

and I think
of an atheist praying
his voice in the dust in the distance
'Our father who art not there...'
I think
of the madness of prophets
who mumble from rags in large cities
of actors at home
practicing Hamlet, practicing Lear
in the mirror, their breath's like a ghost at the window
I've heard Walt Whitman
wagging his beard in my parlour, oh Edison droning
I've heard Yeats
singing his song of old mother, like the sigh
of the wind in a tree
oh, Watson come quickly
I've spilled all our acid
and I think of my bachelor uncle
asleep in his bedroom
with the sound of the ewes
in his bones
I think of their lambing
as the gather of weather in moonlight
I think
of the wasps in the wall at the clinker-built cottage
fanning their hive
in the heat of the summer
of the crystalized cooling of honey
how it whitens like frost
of an autumn

and what might we not do
when we're lonely
too lonely to listen
like the dark from the floor to the ceiling
with rain on a metal roof
booming

John B. Lee

Swearing in Church

We're sitting to supper
at the baby sitter's house
when her parrot
begins to squawk

goddamn kids! goddamn kids!
 goddamn kids! goddamn kids!

and at this refrain

her parrot cursing
like a pirate's shoulder
perseverating on disgruntlement

goddamn kids! goddamn kids!

our hostess
blushing like beet water
forces a smile
that says

how sharply quiet
the taxidermist's fox
how ornithological
the permanent stilling of beaks

and she throws a glance at the perch
as if the bird
might learn about silence
from knives in the night.

nasser hussain

runnning with scissors

It all started with the pepsi. Cam said he'd give me his 600 ml pepsi with the free game piece under the cap which I really needed because I'm only three hundred and seventy five away from the jacket which has a really cool pocket on the shoulder for your pencils and Cam said he would give me the pepsi if I ate glue in art class which is right after lunch and I said okay even though I wasn't very hungry because my dad used to eat paste when he was a kid and he seems pretty much okay now so I drank the pepsi and now I only need three hundred and seventy four more to get the jacket but I might cash them in earlier and get the movie gift certificates because the incredible hulk movie is coming and I don't want to miss it and it would be pretty cool if my dad took me to the theatre and he said "two tickets for the incredible hulk, please" and I could say "excuse me dad, I think you miscounted because I already have the tickets" and then I'd slide my tickets to the ticket taker who would be really impressed and dad would have to spend my ticket money on the extra large combo pack which he says he can't afford and I don't need anyway, but since the hulk is my favorite and dad's got the extra money I figure I can have the extra large combo pack which is a popcorn, twizzlers, nacho chips and cheese, and an extra large pepsi which I share with my dad because it's too heavy at first and besides

it makes me pee which is why I shouldn't have eaten the paste in art class. because it was really slippery and hard to handle and I got it all over my pants, which is bad because dad hates doing the laundry, sometimes I see him turning his undershirts inside out so he can wear them to the office one more time but we're not poor or anything, I get quarters all the time to go to the arcade, but I just save them up so I can take dad to the movies and the zoo, but he's gonna be pretty busy with these pants later on today, you bet. That glue was really sticky and then, as if you can believe it, things got worse. Cam was pretty sure that I was just faking eating the glue so I took a big glop of it and smeared it all over my mouth and gave him my best incredible hulk face. Dad always told me that my face would freeze like that but I never believed him until then. a couple of minutes later and I couldn't move my mouth but since it was art class it didn't really matter if I couldn't open my mouth since all we were doing was gluing these stupid macaroni elbows and old shells onto a piece of paper except for Cam who took a couple of macaroni elbows and shoved them really far up his nose which is something I cant do since it tickles too much and we started laughing except Cam was kind of snorting which was really funny and made me snort too which felt better since I glued my mouth shut and then Mr. Lamarche asked Cam "is everything alright over there, boys?" and Cam tried to say, "Yes, sir" but instead a macaroni elbow came flying out of his nose and hit the blackboard AND IT STUCK which is really grody and everyone started to laugh really hard and yell "boogeroni, boogeroni" and especially when Mr. Lamarche had to clean it off the blackboard so he yelled at everyone, "why can't you behave like Nasser, he's not laughing" which was true because my mouth was pretty well stuck together now, but I had my back to him since the tables are round so he couldn't see my hulk face which was probably good for him because he's pretty old and my dad always has a heart attack or something when I show him the hulk face which is different from the way he looked when I got home

but the boogeroni was really funny, and Cam looked like he did when he had figured a way to get chocolate bars out of the vending machine for free, and he kept looking at the macaroni on the table and whenever he picked one up, he'd bring it close to his nose and make a really retarded face and he'd whisper "who likes boogeroni? everyone like boogeroni..." and I'd have to try really hard not to laugh or I'd

wet my pants. and Mr. Lamarche was really mean about asking for permission to go no matter how bad you had to and this time I had to go really bad so I put up my hand and when Mr. Lamarche said yes, Nasser, what would you like, I couldn't say anything because my lips were stuck together and I still had my hulk face on too which I think really scared Mr. Lamarche, but he really didn't need to be scared because the hulk wouldn't have wanted to hurt Mr. Lamarche unless Mr. Lamarche had a gun or something but I understand why he got scared because I do a pretty good hulk face and then Cam made another batch of boogeroni, but this time it was a double barrel and it hit the windows on the far side of the room where Amanda and Renee were working and one of them bounced off the glass and stuck to Amanda's macaroni ninja and I think the other one went into Renee's hair but nobody's found that one yet and they started screaming and Mr. Lamarche went over to them for a second and I couldn't wait anymore, so I took off for the bathroom as fast as I could and I wish I had made a spiderman face instead of a hulk face because spiderman is really fast, and the hulk is pretty big and slow and when I got there I found out that my pants were glued shut

and even though the hulk is pretty stupid, there's a really smart guy inside of him and I figured out what to do. I ran out of the bathroom and into Mr. Dixon's grade eights where they keep the really sharp scissors, but I think my hulk face really scared them because everyone got really quiet and they just stared at me and even though everyone tells you not to run with scissors I couldn't really help it and ran back to the bathroom with the scissors over my head so I wouldn't poke out my eye if I fell and I cut off my pants and made whizz just in the nick of time.

my dad sometimes tells me that schools nowadays aren't as good as the ones that were around when he was little, but I learned a lot that day. I learned girls don't like boogeroni, too much pepsi makes you need to pee really bad, glue tastes a bit like spearmint, and it's good for keeping your pants up after you cut them off.

f. ward

a pink gun for girls

my four year old daughter
        begged
for this galaxy pistol
hanging in the toy section
of the dollar store

        there she was
snow white butt end
curving sensuously
up to a candy floss shade
of trigger
        attached
to a hot pink 8 shooting
translucent barrel
(all the better to see that
pumping action)

        she came
with an extension
a silencer sort of thing
lace patterned in white
with red tip
all this
        for a buck

        she was
made in china
packaged in france
& easily sold
to us north americans
except for the fact that:

                i am
a politically correct
conscientious citizen/mother
who is supposed to be disgusted
by such merchandise
& therefore dragged
my sceaming child
away from the offending item
& over to the candy isle
where we bought
                a big sucker

for pacification

i snuck back later
& bought it
                for myself
(for educational
& research purposes only
                of course)

i had to know
if the silencer
                really worked

f. ward

the blue van of happiness

pack it up
wake the kids
back it out
are we there yet?
fully loaded
automatic
with a kick-ass
are we there yet?
       stereo
catch the 407
to 400 barrie
are we there yet?
then number 11
are we there yet?
hang a left
at trout creek
are we there yet?
onto the
long & winding
       522
each bend in the road an
are we there yet?
& a town that never changes
all the way to
are we there yet?
       clear lake
& the cottage
my father built
above it all
for about 15 minutes of
       sitting
on the dock of the bay
& a few good vibrations

           in between
smacking deer flies
on blistered shoulders
           intoxicated
with clean air
shimmering water
& mid-day alcohol

then it's time to:

pack it up
wake the kids
back it out
i need to go pee
fully loaded
automatic
with a kick-ass
i need to go pee
           stereo
to the
long and whining
           522
each bend in the road an
i need to go pee
& a rear view town
hang a right
at trout creek
squeeze into
i need to go pee
the heavy metal
convoy
on number 11
stop at every
i need to go pee
on the way back
catch the 407
           ASAP

fuck the 403
i need to go pee
then join the QE
around the big curve
overlooking
      brown bay
through toxic haze
i need to go pee
then exit at
      york blvd.
to downtown hamilton
& a semi-detached
in the middle of it all
      front veranda
littered with sales flyers
& a line up for the toilet

OCT 17/00

Oct. 17/00

Dear Diary:

You won't *believe* what happened to me today!

And all because P. D. (ick) wouldn't hold the elevator for me.

Figures!

Because of *her*, I miss the #403 by one stinking minute and don't get to see Mr. You-Know-Who. Damn that P.D. all to hell!

So I catch the 4:52 and I figure I'll read some of the manual (BO-ring). I sit on a double seat, all by my lonesome, and I put my bag on my lap and my book on my bag and I guess I *must* of snoozed, 'cause next thing I know, we're on the Oak Street Bridge and some good-smelling suit is sitting next to me.

YUM, right?

So there I am, just trying to figure out if I was snoring, or drooling in my sleep, or something *gross* like that, when I figure something in my bag *must* of leaked, 'cause my lap has this real warm spot.

How embarrassing, right?

I pick up just the corner of my bag to have a peak (trying not to let the suit see me do such a hick thing) and it isn't a leak at all –

It's that guy's HAND!!! On my *LAP!*

GROSS!!!

He notices that I clued in and whips his hand away and scratches his ear, real casual. Like, I'm gonna be fooled! I couldn't BELIEVE it!

So I make like that chick on 'True Lies' and I karate-chop him one, right in the old Adam's Apple.

Well.

Guess I got him pretty good, 'cause he falls right outta his seat, into the aisle, choking and grabbing his throat. Just desserts, right?

Next thing you know, some sales guy from The Bay sitting across the aisle jumps up, pulls the suit up off the floor, and gives him the Heimelich maneuver.

The freakin' Heimelich maneuver.

The whole time he's saving the day, the sales guy is shouting at me over the suit's shoulder, "Did it come out yet? Did it come out yet?"

Un-be-LIEV-able.

Then this old broad from the back of the bus comes running up to us, *slaps* the sales guy, and starts screaming away about CPR. I mean, she's *hysterical*! I could see her handprint clear as day on the poor sales guy's face. And the way she's screaming – the only thing I get is we're supposed to lay him down and give him mouth-to-mouth.

Like, *right*, lady. *You* kiss the perv.

Next thing, this other suit is standing there, flapping his arms up and down like a windmill, shouting about extreme allergic reactions and how his middle kid gets them from peanuts. Just the smell of peanuts is enough to choke his middle kid. So he starts frisking the sicko, looking for a reaction kit and – get this – he wants me to open the suit's briefcase and search through there. The whole time, the sicko's making sounds like he ate a Brillo pad or something.

I just couldn't take it anymore. I cracked right up. Laugh? I could of used a Depends. I mean, you should of seen these guys!

And you won't *believe* what happened next:

All those people start yelling at the bus-driver to stop the bus... STOP THE BUS!

And the bus pulls over and they KICK ME OFF! On the HIGH-WAY!

Can you BELIEVE it?

So. It takes me an extra HOUR to walk home and meanwhile Ma is *right* ticked off, 'cause she held dinner and thinks I forgot to call and went out partying or something. Like, *chill*, Ma.

And then I miss America's Most Wanted.

And all because P. D. (ick) wouldn't hold the elevator. I am sooooo mad at her.

Anyhoo. Such is life.

I sure hope Mr. You-Know-Who is on the bus tomorrow.

J. Hugh MacDonald

Attraction

hoping to improve him
she gave her young admirer
a shirt
with "Magnetic Poetry"
embroidered
on its left breast.
Since then
she can't separate him
from her fridge.

J. Hugh MacDonald

What We Say about the Dead

He was dead for two weeks a while ago.
You can hear people talking, you know.
She wasn't sure if he smelled of liquor
or merely human fermentation.
Both, said her friend, the nurse, who'd heard
him too, but later insisted the man
had said "dead for two minutes."
But she claims he said two weeks
so the incident stuck in her memory.
The thought of being dead two weeks
and then coming back after listening
to what people had to say about
you after being dead that long could
change everything. There are things
she would like to know about death
but won't ask this man who once died
for two weeks and is back in "Emerg."
And she intends to be careful what
she says out loud the next time he dies.

Jay Dolmage

Imposing Order III: Marlins/Marlinettes

Dear Parents:

P LEASE TAKE NOTE that despite the circulation of certain unfounded rumors to the contrary, the events of October 31st, 2002 were not the responsibility of Marlins/Marlinettes Swim Club nor of employee Craig Richardson. We've been enjoying having your son/daughter as a member of our swim club. We hope this relationship continues.

Today we're taking the opportunity to state, loud and clear, that we never have and never will allow young swimmers to doff swimgear and perform a "white whale" maneuver. This is not part of the official Marlin/Marlinette curriculum, and any swimmer doffing gear on the deck or in the pool will be severely reprimanded. We have lots of toilets for these children to clean in restitution.

Furthermore, the resale of hyperactivity medication between young Marlins/Marlinettes is a matter that we frown seriously upon. But it is also not something we can go around policing. We have to say it comes down to a transaction between two consenting young adolescents whose parents have or have not instilled in them the proper value system or any values whatsoever. Teaching these values is not in our curriculum.

One thing that is in our curriculum is swimming technique. Which is what you send your son/daughter to us for. If you want ethics, there's a place you can go called Church.

To further address said vicious and ridiculous rumors about the Halloween evening classes under question, we'd like to say that Craig Richardson is himself sorry for the way he behaved. Marlin/Marlinette swim club would also like to say that there will be scheduling changes next year, to ensure that the staff party begins only after the day's lessons are completed, and doesn't start early in the afternoon. We have also removed the audiocassette player from the pool-deck, so that the matter of whether or whether not an instructor's choice of music is appropriate is no longer relevant. Open containers of spirits have always been and will continue to be verboten on the pool-deck.

In terms of addressing some other rumors and insinuations, Craig has brought to our attention several important questions:

1. Was it Craig who took his trunks/suit off in the pool?
2. Was it Craig who, even before he came into the pool area to prepare to enter the pool and later take his trunks/suit off, handed out 350mg tablets of Ritalin in the Boys change-room and received a five dollar payment for every pill? Later giving away the remainder of the Ritalin gratis to various young Marlinettes?
3. Was it Craig who was cavorting on the pool deck to the music and also running and performing other illegal pool deck activities?

   Or, at least, was it Craig who was doing this the most?
4. Was it Craig who, after removing the trunks/suit, performed a non-curricular "white whale"?
5. Finally, was it Craig who forgot to ask his offspring the question "if your swim instructor told you to jump off a cliff would you do it?" In order to reinforce the fact that kids can think for themselves? So that they actually do think for themselves and refuse to do other non-curricular acts that Craig did or did not ask them to do for the rest of the staff to watch?

We think you'll find that the answer to each of the above questions is no. No, it was not Craig Richardson. Furthermore, no, it was not the Marlin/Marlinette Swim Club. In each case it was your kids and/or you.

There are, of course, other questions that could have been asked. One could ask, was Craig in real swim-instructor shape in terms of sobriety? What about the lifeguards, were they in real lifeguard shape in terms of sobriety and not passing out? But we answer these questions with more questions of our own. We wonder, are you the judge of sobriety in terms of are you a sobriety-testing machine? Also, we are to suppose you never imbibe?

Furthermore, there is the matter of your son/daughter and his/her performance of strokes. From now on, let's resolve to focus our attention on swimming. After all, what kind of impression are we giving children when we devote time and energy to discussing and spreading ridiculous rumors? We are giving the impression that swimming is unimportant and that it is okay to have deficient technique. Is this what the majestic Ocean Marlin symbolizes? No.

Rest assured that the young entrepreneur with the ADHD prescription has received a warning. Furthermore, he will not be taking his medication on Marlin/Marlinette lesson nights, so as to avoid the possibility of his 'cheeking' a pill for later resale.

Finally, just so you don't think we forgot, we want to address the issue of the "Haunted Showers". The concept had been to create a 'spooky' atmosphere in the showers by running hot water for fog and removing fuses to maintain darkness. As we understand it, as the students entered the shower area from the pool-deck and staff closed the doors behind them, the effect was indeed spooky. In retrospect, the Marlin Swim Club would have cancelled this activity had it known beforehand the state of inebriation facing both staff and swimmers alike on that particular evening. And with this 20/20 hindsight, we see that we could have avoided many of the more serious accidents—the slipping and the collisions and the slightly greater than first degree burns. But the world we live in happens to be imperfect, by the way. So we won't use our perfect hindsight to question why your child was so quick to panic. Or to focus on analyzing your own parenting in general, which we won't do, in order to keep this letter brief.

In conclusion, the Marlin/Marlinette Swim Club refuses to take any legal responsibility for the events of October 31st, 2002. That said, we look forward to seeing your son/daughter next week, for our Winter Wonderland Holiday Celebration. Students are reminded to bring their Pool Noodles.

Yours Truly,
The Marlin/Marlinette Swim Club

Contributors' Bios

Sylvia Adams is the author of the novel *This Weather of Hangmen,* and of *Mondrian's Elephant* which won the 1998 Cranberry Tree Press poetry chapbook contest. She is instructor/facilitator for two Ottawa poetry groups and editor of two chapbooks for the Field Stone Poets.

Roger Bell resides and writes in the vast uncharted wilderness of Tay Township, where dogs and snowmobiles roam free. He recently edited *Larger Than Life* (Black Moss Press, 2002), an anthology of poetry on the topic of celebrity. He is one of six poets in *Six Voices* (Hidden Brook Press, 2002). His last full book of poetry was *When The Devil Calls* (Black Moss, 2000). He prefers his toast light and his humour dark.

What **Jocko Benoit** is allowed to say about himself is that his poems have appeared or will appear in magazines such as *The Malahat Review, Queen's Quarterly, Event,* and the anthology *Line By Line.* His first book of poetry is *An Anarchist Dream.* He has lived in various parts of Canada – but you can check C.S.I.S. records for further details. He watches the night sky so intently because he has not yet found intelligent life on this planet and really really wants to go home please.

Anne Campbell is a Saskatchewan writer with roots in England and Croatia. She has published four collections of poetry, stories and non-fiction. All explore reconciliation, with self and otherwise. She believes humor contributes greatly to this possibility.

Shannon Cowan has a degree in Visual Arts from the University of Guelph, attended the Banff Centre for the Arts Fall Studio in 1998, and is a three-time delegate to the B.C. Festival of the Arts. Oolichan Books published her first novel, *Leaving Winter,* in 2000 and the novel subsequently made the BC Bestseller List. Shannon currently lives in Sointula, BC where she is completing her Master's Degree in Creative Writing with the University of B.C. She is the recipient of the Eden Mills Literary Prize and has been shortlisted for the CBC Literary Competition.

Jay Dolmage is a student. His fiction has appeared in *Kiss Machine* and is expected to appear in *Tart, The New Quarterly,* and *The Gingko Tree Review* in the near future. Jay sings about robots, raccoons, love, loss and jazz dancing in the band "Finishing School." He thinks that these things are very, very funny: Bob Saget, kittens dressed up in jean jackets, monkeys with hats, karaoke videos, babies that can talk. E-mail him at jaydolmage@aol.com

Marty Gervais is an award-winning poet, journalist and photographer. His poetry has won him the Milton Acorn People's Poetry Award as well as the Habourfront Festival Prize. He was also the recipient of an award in the category of humour with the Western Ontario Newspaper Awards. Marty Gervais has published 12 books of poetry. His *To Be Now: Selected Poems* was released this year. He lives in Windsor, Ontario.

Elizabeth Glenny writes poetry rather than upset her analyst with what is really on her mind. She is plagued by ironic observations of the world disrupting her attempts to write poetry which will be taken seriously. Elizabeth appreciates errors made by editors of *Arachne, Kairos, The New Quarterly, Vintage 99,* and Canadian Authors Association, Niagara Branch for publishing a few of her poems.

Jane Eaton Hamilton is the author of six books, most recently the short story collection *Hunger.* Her work has appeared in such places as the *New York Times, Maclean's, Fine Gardening,* and *Seventeen* magazine as well as in numerous anthologies, and has won the *Yellow Silk* fiction award, the *Paragraph* fiction award, the *Event* non-fiction award, the *Prism* International fiction award, the *Belles Lettres* essay award, the *This Magazine* fiction award and The Canadian Poetry Chapbook Contest. It has also appeared in the *Journey Prize Anthology* and *Best Canadian Short Stories.* It has been cited as distinguished in the Best American Short Stories and was nominated for a Pushcart Prize.

As you read this, **nasser hussain** is pursuing something somewhere.

shereen inayatulla is from Winnipeg but is currently attending the University of Windsor. She is terribly inept at writing her own bio.

Originally from Alberta, **Dale Jacobs** now teaches writing at the University of Windsor. He is the editor of *Ice: New Writing on Hockey* (Spotted Cow Press, 1999). His book of poetry, *Beneath the Horse's Eye* was published in 1997 by Spotted Cow Press. He has also edited *The Myles Horton Reader* (University of Tennessee Press, 2003) and, with Laura Micciche, *A Way to Move: Rhetorics of Emotion and Composition Studies* (Banyon/Cook, 2003). He is currently working on a novel tentatively titled *The Almanac of Longing*.

Hazel Jardine lives, with her husband, in Fort Qu'Appelle, Saskatchewan. She has five children and writes short stories, articles and humorous sketches published in newspapers and magazines throughout North America. Her work is included in several anthologies and has been read weekly on CBC National Radio for two years.

Born and raised on the Prairies, it was not until **Cathy Jewison** moved to the Northwest Territories in 1986 that she turned to creative writing. Since then, her quirky characters have appeared on the pages of *Storyteller* magazine, *Winners' Circle 10,* and *Imprints 11.* Cathy won the 2002 Larry Turner Award for non-fiction from the Valley Writers' Guild.

Gail Johnston alternates between the two worlds which provide the impetus for her writing: Vancouver and Lasqueti Island, BC. Other publications include poems in *Canadian Literature, Contemporary Verse 2,* and, most recently, *The Mentors' Canon.*

Shelley Kozlowski remains a prairie girl at heart, though she currently lives in Vancouver, where she shares an apartment with Miss Kitty, The Uncommonly Large House Cat. She is busy pimping her first novel and spends her free time performing stand-up at local venues.

John B. Lee's work has appeared internationally in over five-hundred magazines, periodicals and anthologies. *The Half-Way Tree* appeared in 2001 from Black Moss Press. In 2002, *In the Terrible Weather of Guns* was published by Mansfield Press. His next book, *Totally Unused Heart,* 2003, was released by Black Moss Press. Lee lives in Brantford, Ontario with his wife Cathy and their two sons, Dylan and Sean-Paul.

Hugh MacDonald writes full time and lives with his wife Sandra, and two of six children, in eastern PEI on the Montague River. He is the author of four books: *Chung Lee Loves Lobsters* (Annick Press, 1992), *Looking for Mother* (Black Moss Press, 1995), *The Digging of Deep Wells* (Black Moss Press, 1997), and *Tossed Like Weeds From the Garden* (Black Moss Press, 1999) He co-edited with Brent MacLaine *Landmarls: An Anthology of New Atlantic Canadian*

Poetry of the Lane (The Acorn Press, 2001), and with Alice Reese *A Bountiful Harvest: Fifteen Years of the Island Literary Awards* (The Acorn Press, 2002). His fourth poetry book from Black Moss, *Cold Against the Heart,* was released in 2003.

Playwright and short-story writer **B.D. (Brian) Miller** lives in Regina. His story "Ivory Majesto's Eye-Poppin', Stomach-Turnin', Faith-Shatterin' Freak Show" first appeared in *Storyteller* magazine, after winning second prize in *Storyteller's* 2000 Great Canadian Story Contest. His one-act comedy, "Dumpster Diving," received a public, staged reading as part of Globe Theatre Regina's 2002 On The Line Cabaret, and premiered at the 2003 On The River's Edge Literary and Performing Arts Festival in North Battleford. For production rights to "Dumpster Diving" (or to say hello), please contact the author at: miller@millwrite.com

Gina Rozon is a freelance writer living in La Ronge, Saskatchewan. Her humour columns have been appearing bi-weekly in the *La Ronge Northerner* since 1999 and on CBC Radio One, Regina since 2001. She can be reached by email at mgrozon@sk.sympatico.ca

Bob Stamp is a Calgary writer of poetry and prose. His poems have appeared in *Alberta Views, Freefall, Green's Magazine, The Prairie Journal of Canadian Literature,* and in the anthologies *Wr[ink]le* (Calgary: 2001), *Crossing Place* (Red Deer: 2002) and *Conjunction* (Calgary: 2002).

Richard Stevenson lives in Lethbridge, AB and teaches Canadian Literature, Creative Writing, and Business Communication for Lethbridge Community College. He has published thirteen collections of poetry and has two more forthcoming in 2003: *A Tidings of Magpies: Haiku, Senryu, and Tanka* from Spotted Cow Press in Edmonton and *Take Me To Your Leader!,* YA verse from Bayeux Arts Inc. in Calgary.

f. ward is a writer and visual artist who was born in Manchester, UK and emigrated to Canada as a child. Most of her adult life has been "spent" in Hamilton, Ontario. Her poetry appears in various anthologies and journals including most recently the anthology of "the best in Canadian poetry" entitled *Oval Victory* (edited by Linda Rogers). She is the author of a two chapbooks of poetry and images; *side effects* and *Life & Ledger.*

Publication Credits

Some of the writing in *North by North Wit* has previously appeared in the following venues.

"Being Jane Hamilton," by Jane Hamilton, was previously published in *Grain* (Summer 2002).

"Dumpster Diving," by B.D. Miller, received a staged reading as part of Globe Theater Regina's On The Line Cabaret (February 2002) and was produced by the On The River's Edge Literary and Performing Arts Festival in North Battleford, Saskatchewan (February 2003).

"For This, You Need a University Degree?," by Gina Rozon, was previously published in the *La Ronge Northerner* (April 9, 2002) and aired on CBC Radio One, Regina (April 2002).

"Ivory Majesto's Eye-Poppin', Stomach-Turnin', Faith-Shatterin' Freak Show," by B.D. Miller, was previously published in *Storyteller* (Summer 2000).

"Pumpin' Gas," by Anne Campbell, was previously published in *Grain* (Winter 1998).

"Sans Lemon Grass," by Elizabeth Glenny, was previously published in *Outreach Connection* (Novemeber 21, 2000).

"Unhinged," by Shelley Kozlowski, was previously published in *Stitches, The Journal of Medical Humour* (March 2001).

"Vacuum Fall-Out" by Hazel Jardine was previously published in the *Saskatoon Star Phoenix* and broadcast on CBC radio.